OLD WEIRD South

New stories of the eerie,
macabre, supernatural,
and spooky from the
American South

Edited by Tim Westover

QW PUBLISHERS

2013

The Old Weird South

Copyright ©2013 by QW Publishers, LLC

QW PUBLISHERS, LLC
Grayson, GA USA
www.QWPublishers.com

ISBN: 978-0-9849748-1-8

First edition published in 2013 by Q W Publishers

Introduction ©2013 by Tim Westover | "Ghost Dog of Georgia" ©2013 by A. Camille Renwick | "To Gnaw the Bones of the Wolf-Mother" ©2013 by Sean Taylor | "Yalobusha County, 1862" ©2013 by Ken Teutsch | "Yankees in Georgia: Chasing Ghosts and the General along the Old W&A Railroad" ©2013 by Lewis Powell IV | "A Hunnerd Dollars, Gold" ©2013 by Peter Mehren | "The South, Rise Again" ©2013 by DL Thurston | "The Dragon and the Shark" ©2013 by David Boop | "Matty and the Grey Man" ©2013 by Lara Ek | "Railroad Bill" ©2013 by Janice Croom | "Passage" ©2013 by Daniel Powell | "The Devil at the Crossroads" ©2013 by Wenonah Lyon | "A Busy Day for the Bayou Banshee" ©2013 by Herb Shallcross | "The Spook Light" ©2013 by Jay Rogers | "That Damned Game" ©2013 by Kristina R. Mosley | "Tennessee Ghosts" ©2013 by Stephen Newton | "The Gift of Understanding" ©2013 by Sherry Fasano | "Bradford House" ©2013 by Laura Haddock | "Storm Fronts" ©2013 by Michael Hodges | "The Healer" ©2013 by Josh Strnad | "A True Story about the Devil and Jamie's Shoes" ©2013 by Megan Engelhardt | "Murdock" ©2013 by Chris Dezarn | "Underwater" ©2013 by Erin Mundy | "The End of Grace" ©2013 by Meriah Lysistrata Crawford | "Florida Natural" ©2013 by Ben Bowlin

Contents

Introduction

In the modern South, we are not generally a superstitious lot. The ways of the world have crowded out the daily doings of haints and spooks, and we don't ascribe much power or agency to the forces that once were integral to the worldview of our forebearers.

But we still know ghosts.

My mother remembers a rocking chair that moved on its own—it should have been a reassuring presence, symbolizing for her a connection to her grandmother, but it still sent an icy shiver through her.

Two of my friends encountered one of St. Augustine's old specters on their wedding night. When they mentioned her at checkout, the clerk brushed it off as a regular occurrence, just one of the hazards (or perks) of staying at a historic hotel.

The cute tea shop in Lawrenceville, Georgia, has its own resident phantom, the shade of a little girl that must have somehow been connected to the time when Honest Alley was a mule market with a tough reputation. This ghostly girl was never much trouble for anyone; her footsteps and her otherworldly laughter were only curiosities.

I don't myself hold with the existence of ghosts—I've never seen or felt one—but I couldn't stay late at the tea shop, as the Earl Grey cooled and the candles sputtered, without ... wondering.

I think, though, that we are not haunted by ghosts as much as we are haunted by the past. Something greater and grander used to be here, but also something darker—something that I would not wish to return to.

For all its antebellum romance and natural beauty, the South has known more suffering than most places in the United States. There is blood on the land—the victims were Native Americans, slaves and freedom fighters, soldiers North and South, modern martyrs for civil rights and equality. Perhaps these two currents—the noble past and the tumultuous past—mix and swirl and clash like storm fronts, and the lightning and thunder reveal the ghosts in our shadows and stories.

This anthology is not a collection of real-life happenings, but it intends to show the broader role of the supernatural in Southern storytelling. I've selected original stories that approach the supernatural in a variety of ways. Campfire stories that are meant for a scare. Family stories that preserve a particular incident or oddity through the generations. A few nonfiction pieces that call out moments of Southern history and the supernatural fingers that intertwine with it: the hijacking of the General, the murder of Grand Ole Opry star Stringbean, and the drownings in Atlanta's Lake Lanier, where speedboats float above old farms and fence posts. Some stories included here take a folk idiom, like the devil at the crossroads, and give it a clever spin. And there are, of course, literary tales. The South's great writers have never shied away from the ghosts of the past.

While most of the stories are set in the Deep South (and in particular, Georgia, which is my home state), I've reached further afield, selecting stories from Florida, Missouri, and even Oklahoma, whose Southern connection is bolstered by its Cherokee population. They are arranged roughly chronologically, beginning with Cherokee-inspired tales, then moving to the Civil War and up to the present day. It's been my honor to work with these twenty-four different authors—many of them Southern, but some hailing from as far away as Canada, the UK, and China.

Tim Westover
Lawrenceville, Georgia

Ghost Dog of Georgia

Camille Alexa

The dog smells burning.

The dog has caught whiffs of ash and smoke all morning, but a shift in the wind over the top of the ridge makes it seem suddenly very close. He's accustomed to the fires of the people with whom he travels. Together, he and the people wander the meandering river valley and the flat meadow plains, once even touching the ocean, vast and briny, scented like salt and sex and the color blue. Where there are humans, there's always fire, always: they use it to harden bone and wood and shard to fashion the weapons they toss at larger prey; they use it to dry the scraped-clean hides they wear slung low around their middles; they use it to bake clay and they sear animal innards with it, and afterward they toss the dog the bones; and when it's cold they huddle near the fire and invite the dog to join. They use fire so often, it's as much a part of the dog's coexistence with them as is the warm feeling low under his ribs when they bend to pat his shaggy haunch in passing or gently stroke the thick ruff around his neck.

Some nights the dog lies awake listening to the howls of others more like himself, swiveling his pointed ears to catch the eerie wailing under the round white moon, wails of loss and challenge and joy over unknowable things which the dog can't know because he chooses instead to live with humans.

Two toddlers, each half his size, roll toward him across the flattened yellow morning grass. They're so bare and small, so vulnerable without fur. The dog lies still as they climb over him, their soft, feeble limbs pummeling his thick coat in play.

Warm in the sun, he closes his eyes and is able to forget his unease over the scent of distant ash as the child-people laugh and tug his ears and finally curl up against him to fall asleep, skin pressed to fur pressed to skin.

The dog wakes to pandemonium. The toddlers have been snatched from his sides, the rough motion of their departure and their keening wails of protest adding to the panic in the meadow. People cry out to each other in shrill, shallow voices, grabbing with panicked carelessness their children and the small essentials they carry from camp to camp, from forest to field to swamp. Burning clogs the dog's nose and coats the back of his throat as the meadow's dry yellow grasses crackle, flaring up on all sides at once. The scent had increased so gradually and had been so familiar, the dog is caught as much by surprise as are the people around him.

He chooses one of his favorites among the people, a slender human female taller than many of the men in her pack, and trots alongside her as she stumbles, coughing, past a burning clump of brush higher than her head, one of his afternoon-nap companions wailing under each of her arms. The sling she usually carries the infants in is gone, lost in the thickening smoke which stings the dog's eyes and makes his tongue thicken in his mouth as he pants against the gusting heat.

Soon, the dog is leading the woman rather than the other way around. The smoke is too thick to see through, too thick almost to breathe. No sooner does the dog decide on the safest route to lead them from the smoke than the wind shifts again, and a wall of heat and yellow flames springs up to block their path. The summer grasses which had smelled so sweet and seemed so harmless rippling earlier in the morning breeze that flapped across the drowsy meadow have become a sudden enemy, fuel for flames. The dog thinks of the coolness of the vast ocean he once saw, recalls the feeling of swift river-water running over his scorched paws, of clear sparkling rain falling on his smoking coat.

The coughing woman at his heels staggers and drops to her knees. The toddlers clutched under her arms are motionless, eyes closed and tiny mouths slack. The dog barks at the humans. Barking, barking. He will save them. He will.

When the woman slumps completely to the ground, the dog clamps his teeth on her wrist and drags.

The last thing the dog knows is the tang of the woman's blood in his mouth, the first human blood he has ever tasted, saturated with the flavor of his own failure to save her from the flames roaring in his ears, blinding him, searing his lungs from the inside with each burning breath he draws.

The dog smells burning.

The night is dark, but it seems to have been dark for a very long time. If the dog counted things like *months* and *years*, he'd understand the concept of *millennium*; that's how much time has passed on the ridge south of the river near which a bonfire illuminates a girl surrounded by four laughing men. The dog has no name for the river, but the girl calls it by a word the descendants of those laughing men will one day twist into *Chattahoochee*.

The girl is tall and slender, her long black hair twined into matching plaits falling to each side of her face. She reminds the dog of the human woman whose blood he can no longer taste on his tongue, but whose last moments he tastes in his heart like a poison flower.

One of the men reaches for the girl. She bites his hand. He jumps back and howls while his fellows point and laugh some more. The night is made blacker by the flickering white light of the bonfire. Another man grasps the girl's arms from behind, and as she kicks and struggles, two others each grip one of her ankles and lower her to the ground. She does not scream or shout, but the dog reads panic in the thrashing of her limbs, smells the sour scent of her fear rising on heated currents along with downy ash from the flames.

The dog bounds from the trees—trees that hadn't existed on this meadow the last time he drew smoke-tinged air into his lungs. He feels himself growing more solid as he runs, feels his fur thickening and his blood quickening in his veins. When did he last have veins and blood and fur? The last time fire on this meadow mingled in the air with human pain.

His body slams into the man with a violence that takes the others by surprise. Their cries spill into the night as they drop the dark-haired woman. The men's hair glints gold and orange in firelight, strange colors like sunset and straw. Other than the braided twists, the girl's hair is like that of other humans the dog has seen before. She smells just as he remembers people smelling too, like forest and river and tall summer grasses.

The girl scrambles to the dog's side as he bares his fangs at her tormentors. One man grabs a burning brand from the fire and thrusts it at the dog. The dog sees the glowing red coals of his pupils reflected in the humans' eyes, the ghostly blue nimbus of his fur and the opalescent gleam of teeth longer and sharper than he'd ever had in life. Another man raises a black metal stick and points it. The girl cringes, her fear striking at the dog like the fangs of a snake. He leaps at the man and feels a buzz and tingle pass through his chest at the first bang and the next.

For the second time the dog tastes human blood, his teeth sinking into the man's shoulder. Bones crunch deep inside. The man cries out to his departing pack, but they are running, running into the trees. After a last shake and growl, the dog lets him go, and he struggles to his feet and staggers after them, his black metal bang stick dragging in the dirt by his side like a broken limb.

The dog turns and trots back to the fire. The girl kneels before him, bows low with arms spread and hands cupped, and breathes a single word: *ofi'*. Though her language didn't exist in the world last time he walked it, he knows, even as he sees himself dissipating into mist against the flickering firelight reflected in her eyes, that the word she whispers to him is *dog*.

Pvt. Seth Anthony Jenkins—née Sarah Anne Jenkins—draws a ragged breath into her bruised lungs, smelling burning metal as Union cannons fire another round. Jenkins thought Peachtree Creek was bad, but Lt. Gen. John Bell Hood has gone and done himself one better here in Atlanta. Jenkins presses her fist harder against the blood welling from her side and closes her eyes to block the sight of a dead soldier a few feet away. She'd turn her head if she could, though the horse wailing its agonies in the bloody mud to her other side would surely be even more distressing than the empty open eyes of her fellow soldier.

This sure isn't how Jenkins pictured it when she sheared her hair off in the cowshed, stole Jimmy's Sunday best clothes, and marched down to the recruiting tent and made her mark, *SAJ*, proud of how she could form actual letters while so many of the other boys in line just put an X beside their names. But her mama had been from Texas and had always said no child of hers was going to run around as ignorant as a Georgia farmer's child, not knowing even how to print her letters. Sarah Anne never had the patience to sit still and learn to string all those letters together like her brother William had, but she sure knew enough to write her monogramme.

A riderless horse thunders up, rising out of the noise and smoke like a ghostly spirit, eyes white and rolling, nostrils black and flared. Its flank and empty saddle are sprayed with human blood, crimson and slick. Jenkins squeezes her eyes shut as the massive iron-shod hooves come near her head, thinking it will be a relief to stop having to hold her own guts in place. A crushed-in skull would be a quick way to go. Quicker than dying of a belly wound in the mud outside Atlanta, surrounded by men who've already given up the ghost, butternut uniforms and blue ones indistinguishable under the muck of battle.

The terrified horse's hooves pass so close, Jenkins feels the short fine bristles on her scalp tingle with the electricity of their nearness, like how wearing a clean woolen skirt on a cold winter day will sometimes generate a spark or make your hair stand on end. It seems a lifetime ago since Sarah Anne has worn a skirt, though she's only been marching with the Army of the Confederate States of America for six months. Six months, and nobody ever caught scent of her as a girl, and now they're going to find out when she's dead and can't have nothing to say about it.

After flying over close enough to ruffle her lashes, the horse disappears again into the billowing smoke. Atlanta's burning, Hood having set fire to the supply depots and to eighty-one ammunition cars to keep them from falling into Union hands. Jenkins isn't sure exactly how many soldiers have died this day, but it's in the thousands. Thousands and thousands, on both sides; she's fixing to be one of them, so she ought to know. She's slightly cheered by the thought that maybe they won't discover her secret after all. Maybe that fire burning Atlanta to the ground will just keep burning—burn through the buildings and the trees, burn the bloody grass meadow, scorch her flesh clean to its bones and then to ash, and leave nothing behind to say she was ever anything but Seth Anthony Jenkins, aged seventeen, big-hipped for a boy but as scrawny as the rest of them and a better shot with a rifle than most. Her daddy taught her that last bit before he went off to volunteer back in '61 right after Jefferson Davis made things official. William didn't wait too long to follow after him, and then it was just Mama and Sarah Anne left behind with only little Jimmy and the dog, Rascal, to look out for them.

Well, Jenkins doesn't regret stealing trousers and signing up. She misses her mama a little, though she could never be the girl her mama wanted. She certainly doesn't miss the skirts and the cooking and the strangulating unfreedom of being a woman, but she does miss her mama, and her dog. She loved that dog.

Sarah Anne is mortified to feel tears sliding down her grimy cheeks. All these months of fighting and eating sawdust and marching her feet bloody and raw without a single tear. And now, when she's about to die with her perfect record intact, her eyeballs start leaking over a big old dog.

She clutches her belly tight with both hands as the sobs wrack her, rifle forgotten or lost someplace in the choking smoke and the smell of gunpowder and metal and death. She hears guns still pounding, but farther off. Everybody in her vicinity is past groaning or moaning, even the poor horse at last, thank goodness. Sarah Anne never could bear to see an animal in pain.

When she opens eyes bleared up with tears and dirt, she smiles, thinking her time has come. Rascal was an old dog when she left; he must've passed over to the other side by now. She knows he did because there he is, padding toward her through a gap in the smoke of battle.

"Hey there, ol' Rascal," she croaks when he stops to stand over her. "Nice to see you. You're such a good boy. Always were."

She raises one bloody hand from her side, keeping the other balled tight and pressed hard to staunch the blood. She reaches for his muzzle, her fingers seeming to pass right through, not connecting with anything, but moving the particles in the air so the thick grey smoke swirls and the dog's image shimmers. But she tries again and this time her hand meets solidity, fur rougher and more wiry than she remembers, ears more pointy and more wide.

"You're not Rascal . . ." Her voice rakes her parched throat. The dog licks her face, and her vision clears. For a heartbeat she'd imagined herself at the farm back home, just lazing in the field with her dog instead of stirring the boiling pot of laundry her mama always had her help Jimmy with on account of him being so small. But it's not Jimmy staring lifeless at her from a few feet away, but some poor farmer's child like her, Confederate or Union, doesn't matter, dead, and probably far from home like her. And it's not Rascal she's staring up at, but some barrel-chested wolflike thing with a strange mottled coat like nothing she's ever seen. His eyes glow at her past the smoke and the distant shouting and the scent of burning that always accompanies a battle.

The dog nuzzles her hand before bending down and grabbing a mouthful of the butternut wool of her coat. His jaws clamp firm but gentle on the homespun fabric, and he begins to drag her through the grass and mud, away from the fire and smoke.

Sarah Anne loses consciousness between one blood-filled gully and the next, but when she opens her eyes, it's to the white canvas ceiling of a medical tent. Her body is pleasantly numb where morphine floods her veins, her mind floating too far away to be more than mildly alarmed when the doctor, with his fancy moustache and Union-blue trousers and grimy white apron, leans over her.

"You've pulled through, I see," he says. "I'm sure your mother will be glad to have you back. I take it she's already lost a son to this war? A brother you might've stolen some clothes from in order to sign up?"

Sarah Anne notices for the first time her nakedness beneath the sheets. Well, not naked: bandages wrap her in what feels like a hundred different places from knee to neck. "Jimmy," she says, her throat still rougher than burlap. "I took Jimmy's Sunday best."

The doctor studies her, squints before nodding, then wipes his hands on his blood-smeared apron. "Well, you've got the grit, I'll give you that," he says. "Few soldiers wearing a uniform of any color with a puncture the size of yours and all those burns could've dragged themselves up that ridge to my infirmary tent. If you hadn't, you'd be dead like the other twelve thousand poor souls."

The doctor moves away to check another patient's pulse, and Sarah Anne watches sunlight dapple the canvas ceiling overhead and notes the absence of pounding guns and knows Atlanta is lost, and the South is lost, but most of all she knows her secret is lost and she is a girl again.

The dog smells burning.

His lungs expand into being, drawing deep the scents of fire and danger and humans in need. The meadow and the ridge, as always, are vastly different from the last time the dog saw them. Gone is the acrid fire billowing into the air, coming from all directions at once and from none. Gone is the artificial thunder rumbling as the dog had never heard it before, rolling across the plain covered in smoke and dead horses and ten thousand dying boys. In place of blood-churned mud is an endless expanse of flat grey rock, smooth and rough at the same time beneath paws which grow more solid with each footfall.

He's slightly disoriented by the many lights glittering in the darkness glittering brighter than stars above but without heat, without smoke. The heat and smoke come from the human dwelling on the other side of the flat stone river, roiling silently out into the cool night.

The dog pads quickly across the unfamiliar smooth stone, ducking between two hulking hollow metal boulders smelling strangely of battle, of ozone and old coal. Doesn't matter. He knows what has drawn him here, what always draws him to this place; inside that human dwelling are a man and a woman and their two children. They sleep, not knowing the breath in their lungs will soon be replaced with smoke if not for the dog coming from so far away to wake them, to lead them from the burning and the fire and the death.

Briefly, the dog is filled with the memory of that perfect day an aeon ago—though of course the dog doesn't know *aeons*. At this moment, as his shadowy form passes through the flimsy artificial wood of a suburban dwelling, what the dog knows is the memory of that morning of perfect happiness when he lay on his side on packed earth, two human toddlers tugging his ears in play before curling into his warmth so the three of them could sleep in the sunshine, breathing the distant scent of ash carried from over the ridge on gentle summer breezes.

To Gnaw the Bones of the Wolf-Mother

Sean Taylor

It was supposed that lost spirits were roving about everywhere in the invisible air, waiting for children to find them if they searched long and patiently enough.

—Mourning Dove (Christine Quintasket), Salish

The words of my people are all I have. They are law to me. In those words, I am called Wolf Cub with Child Eyes. But today is the day I become a man, and then my people will know me by another name—a name neither they nor I know yet.

A name Yowa will choose for me, a name the wilderness will prove is mine.

Then my name will also be law, even as my people are known by our name—the Aniyunwiya.

"Cub," my father says to me. "Today, you are still a boy. You must be ready."

"I am ready," I tell him, "to be a man."

He laughs. "Patience, Cub." His eyes turn down, dark and serious. "Your quest will be dangerous. Some boys do not return."

"And they go to Yowa, Father."

"Yes," he says and nods like one of the white settlers below, low in the valleys, afraid to live higher because of the wolves and other beasts. "But I am not eager for you to go that far away yet. I would have more time with you here in our home."

"And I would sooner die than fail to become a man."

He laughs and grips my shoulder with one calloused hand. "Then you are almost a man already."

The warriors have gathered in a circle outside our hut, and my father leads me out to join them. The oldest of them, a grey-haired man of wrinkles and a back bent like a curve in a river, stands with the aid of a staff and points to me. "Come, Wolf Cub with Child Eyes," he says.

And I do, leaving my father to take his place in the circle of warriors.

The old one, who is called Leader by law but Gentle Bear by the men of the tribe, crouches down on one knee beside the fire and bids me sit in front of him. He reaches into his shirt and retrieves a pipe. I look back at my father, who ignores me and chants softly with the other men. Gentle Bear pushes a branch into the fire and holds it there until it burns, then shoves the flaming end into the open mouth of the pipe. Smoke billows up from it, and a pungent smell makes me shiver and cough.

Gentle Bear laughs, then tells me that a man could inhale the smoke without coughing like a child. He offers the pipe to me, and I take it. The men around us chant louder:

> *May Yowa speak to this boy and make him a man.*
> *May the winds and the rains challenge this boy and make him strong.*
> *May the beasts torment this boy and make him brave.*
> *May Yowa speak and bring this boy back to us a man.*

Having witnessed the ceremony many times before from the door of our hut, I know what to do, and I rest the mouthpiece of the pipe between my lips. I take a deep breath, then let it go. The wind kisses the back of my neck where my hair is tied into a single braid by leather strips. A beast howls in the far-off woodlands. The fire beside me crackles.

And I suck the pungent smoke into my chest.

I want to cough.

I want to cry.

But a man can inhale the smoke without coughing like a child.

The wait seems to last the rest of the night, but I know it is only a few moments, and eventually, Gentle Bear rises and pulls me up by my hand.

Standing comes to me with more difficulty than before. My body seems to have lost the ability to balance, and my legs seem to be as heavy as the stones that change the river's course.

But Gentle Bear is not challenged by my sudden weakness. He simply holds my arm high, and the warriors break the circle and walk by me in single file, each clasping my arm and smiling as he passes.

The night around me is cold. The ground beneath me is colder still. But the world is quiet, save for the pounding of my heart in the darkness.

I sit atop the mound my people call Elder Home because they believe it is where we originated in the days of our ancestors long past, when the beetle brought the mud to the surface and made the earth. Some have preferred to believe we are descended from the *Tsul Kalu*, the hairy men who came from the darkness of the swamps and learned to create tools and hunt and work the land.

I sit in a darkness that is darker still than the night alone. A skill I learned from my father. Having tied a leather strip around my eyes before the night was complete, I now train my eyes to become like those of the owl and the night creatures. Blindness for a season so that I may see truer when the test of manhood is upon me.

Listening to the wind shriek and the creatures walk about below me, I notice they occasionally stop to moan or growl at each other.

I am safe on the ground, knowing the trees are near enough to climb should one of the beasts wander too near, but each time they speak, my blindness causes me to shudder as though the beasts were encircling me at arm's reach.

When they at last die down and wander off, I wait again for Yowa to visit and give me a vision of my quest. I have heard from other boys who became men that Yowa does not speak to all boys and that some of them only pretend and make up a quest so they can return to the tribe.

But I will wait.

I will not disappoint Yowa when she comes. I will not lie about my quest. I will wait until she speaks. I will wait until my body dies and I hear her with spirit ears.

If I must, perhaps I can stay awake for seven nights, like the panther and owl, and receive the reward of night vision along with them.

As I wait, I tell the night the stories my father and grandfather told to me.

> *A warrior traveled far from the mountains, deep into the swamps to hunt. On the first night of the hunt, the forest remained silent and still. On the second night, it remained the same. On the third night, the warrior cried out to Yowa to provide prey he could hunt to feed his family. On the fourth night, while the warrior was sleeping, he was awakened by the sound of footsteps from the brush.*
>
> *He grabbed his bow and crouched behind a rock. From the leaves, a giant from the tribe of hairy men in the forest backed into the clearing.*

But this was from the time before our people knew the Tsul Kalu.

The warrior silently thanked Yowa. Then he quietly retrieved an arrow from his quiver, notched it into his bow, and drew back the string.

The hairy man turned around and waved his huge arms at the warrior, and the warrior let go of the string. The arrow flew true and pierced the hairy man through his heart, and the giant fell dead on the spot.

The warrior yelled a triumphant cry and leaped from the safety of his rock, thanking Yowa loudly. He used all his strength to drag the heavy body near the fire, and only when the light of the flames were able to help him see did he notice that the giant's hand was clasped around the leg of a hug elk, dead from a blow to its head.

And the warrior grew silent.

Then he cursed his eagerness and his inability to understand. The hairy man was bringing him a gift of food from Yowa. The warrior drew his knife and placed it down onto the middle fingers of his drawstring hand, and he sliced them off then burned the wound in the fire to stop the bleeding.

From that day, my people's ancestors learned to share the land in peace with the hairy men.

Sounds of padded paws return near me, and I listen, still refusing to remove the blindfold. I will only take it off when the time is right, when the test begins in earnest, when I will prove that I will not disappoint Yowa.

There is a loud howl in the distance, not like that of a wolf, but of something malignant, something living by instincts it wasn't born with. Perhaps this night will bring me face-to-face not only with Yowa but also the evil creature my father calls the Wendigo.

The creature is not one my own people speak of. The beast has only been known to us since the time of my father's father, when a warrior from the north—lost and removed from his own Anishinabe people, wandering as his own quest commanded—told us the story of the creature so loathed by even Yowa herself.

I speak the story to the night to quiet my spirit.

> *A long time ago, it is said, long before my father's father's father, my people's ancestors were noble and pure. They lived as one with the creatures and beasts, both the intelligent ones and the natural ones, often playing games with Fox and Bear and Eagle, all the while hunting the elk and the squirrel.*
>
> *But one day, when Fox and his people were starving, they refused to learn how to cultivate grain and identify the healthy berries and leaves, insisting on maintaining their meals of meat and blood alone, no matter that the dumb animals had hidden for the winter or had been run off to lands where they would not be hunted.*
>
> *In a fit of anger, Fox lashed out at his mate and killed her. He carried her body into a cave to hide from the eyes that see everything, and there, he quietly consumed every part of her, even the bones.*
>
> *After that, Fox grew more and more violent, and he taught other foxes how to hunt their own kinds. But Coyote and Bear knew that Fox had to be stopped before he desecrated the land and all its peoples, both with fur and without it. When Fox heard that Bear and Coyote were hunting him, he used his magic to blind the eyes of my people's ancestors to believe they saw him as a wise man of many years, and they allowed him into their tribe and hid him.*

Fox lived in his new tribe for many years, never growing older, and one day, the elders of the people asked him to give away his secret for long life.

It was the moment Fox had been waiting for, and he taught the tribe how to hunt and kill other tribes of men and to eat their meat and use their bones for tools.

But because man was not made of magic like Fox, man was defiled by eating the meat of man, and all who did withered and shriveled and became like walking dead men, and they were cast out of the tribe along with Fox.

They still roam the nights, seeking to turn men into monsters like themselves, possessing them when they do.

My people call them Wendigo, the evil spirits of those who eat the flesh of their own kind.

As I recite the legend, I hear the wanderer's voice reminding me that any man can become Wendigo, that no man is above the desecration, that even good men of his own family had been possessed by the evil when food is scarce. And I see my father grip my shoulder and tell me to remember this before he smiles and tells me to join the other boys playing in the river.

The howl returns, nearer, though still a long way off, and I see past the memories and stories to find myself in the forest again. The padded paws of the curious lesser beasts stop to show respect to the sound. I stand, not removing the blindfold, and hear even the curious creatures scamper away. After a few silent moments, I realize I am alone again.

Another malignant howl, and it fades into a shriek that makes my bones rattle. A boy can be brave enough to face the wolf and even the bear and perhaps even the old man of the forest if Yowa wills it, but no boy has ever had the misfortune to see a Wendigo.

And if the words of the wanderer still run true, no boy, even one on the night of becoming a man, could encounter one and live to tell his adventure.

My heart pounds like ceremonial drums. My ears grow full with the sound. My skin steals the chill from the night wind and takes it deep into my body.

But I do not remove the blindfold.

Nor do I run.

If I am to die tonight, then I will die like a man.

Limbs break behind me, and dead leaves crack on the ground as something quiet walks across them.

Another howling shriek rises in the distance.

The leaves grow silent again.

I wait.

I wait until my heart-drums stop reminding me of my fear.

I wait until my ears empty and become restful.

I wait until the chill warms and my body resists the cold again.

I wait until my legs tell me I should sit down.

And I wait until the quiet around me tells my eyes to close.

A snarl in my ear wakens me. The hot, wet breath tickles the tiny hairs on my neck. Something slick drips onto the bottom of my ear.

And the snarl growls into my ear again. My hand is on my knife before I even think of removing the blindfold.

I lay still.

The breath leaves my neck and finds my cheek instead. The slickness drips onto my cheek and then my chin. The breath reeks of raw meat and dirty water.

I pull the knife free and grip it tightly.

The creature above me growls and presses one sharply clawed paw on my chest.

Instinct drives me as I throw my left arm around its neck without having to remove the blindfold. I twist and pull the thing with the matted fur to the ground beside me and raise my right arm, then I strike like a flash of lightning, driving the knife into the soft part of its chest.

The creature yelps and grabs my wrist with its teeth, wrenching the knife away. I hear it clink against some stones a few feet away as I rip the blindfold away to finally see what manner of beast I am battling.

A wolf. Large and brown, with a single stripe of black wrapping around its back and haunches. A she-wolf.

Regret clutches me, and I look around the forest, searching for cubs. How will Yowa make me a man when I am merely a cub that kills the mother of another?

I see no cubs, and I feel better. Perhaps the she-wolf is Yowa's challenge, and I have passed. Perhaps I was not to receive a vision but to be tested, as others of the tribe have said of their quest. Perhaps my night is over, and I am free to return home and share the blood of this mighty beast with the other warriors I have become a part of.

The beast lets go of my wrist and cocks its head to face me. The brown eyes, large and wet and shining, lock on to mine, and it opens its maw and closes it again. Then again.

Then it snarls one last time, and the head slumps to the dirt and falls still.

I crawl the distance to retrieve the knife, then stand and throw back my shoulders to let the forest know I have become a man, a warrior. I have killed a she-beast while blind.

The leaves and branches crackle and break behind me.

I turn, legs bent and ready, arms at my side, knife in my hand again, my own claw.

Two red eyes stare at me from the darkness. Even with my eyes keen to the darkness, the figure that behind the shining eyes is dark enough to fade into the night air and remain unseen.

"Child Eyes," comes a whisper to my left. "The Wolf Cub that kills its mother."

I spin to where the voice came from, ignoring for the moment the wild red eyes. "What are you!" I yell. "I wasn't afraid of the wolf, and I'm not afraid of you."

"You had no reason to be afraid of the wolf," the voice says.

I look up into the trees. The voice is high.

"Look for me and find me. You look to the Yowa, but I have prayed to her too, and she has given you to me, Cub."

"I thought you a spirit, but you sound like a man. Who are you?"

"I am no spirit, but I am not a man either."

"Then what are you?"

"I am what you came to the forest seeking, boy."

I can hear the madness in the voice's gritted words.

"I'm not afraid of you."

"That is good, Cub. Then you will die brave."

I remember the red-eyed creature and glance to see if it is still watching. A boy fighting one man is a challenge of its own, but fighting one man while worrying about another enemy joining the battle is something that even my father's training hasn't prepared me for.

But the eyes are gone.

I smile.

"Then I will die with honor, Creature Who Is Not Man Nor Spirit."

No response.

"Are you afraid?"

Still no answer.

"No." The words come soft, low, and directly into my ear on a cool breath.

Before I can spin around, a hairy disjointed arm has my throat all but crushed. Claws rake across my stomach, and I yelp as they slash deep gashes into my skin. Blood flows freely across my abdomen.

"I will feast on your flesh, Cub." The claws stop moving and instead begin to dig the gashes, cutting into muscle and gut. "And then I will gnaw the bones of your wolf-mother."

The creature removes its claws from my gut and tosses me away. I hit the ground on my side and roll over onto my stomach. My guts threaten to spill to the ground.

"You taste like life," the creature whispers.

Raising my head, I give my eyes a moment to react to the pain and take in the sight of my attacker. A tall beast, standing on two legs like a bear—no, dressed in the skin of a bear, down to the claws that it wears like a new set of hands. Beneath the bearskin, the creature is filthy—a dark lanky thing caked in dirt and what my nose tells me must be animal waste.

As it grins, I see teeth sharp and stained red.

"You smell like death."

"I am death."

I shake my head. "No. I know what you are. You used to be a man, but you are no longer. You are now a thing of evil, cursed by Yowa."

The thing steps toward me, and I back away one step for each step it takes.

"You are frightened, Cub."

My back bumps against a tree, and I realize I have nowhere else to go, that my stomach risks ripping open the longer I fail to wrap it in buckskin, that the evil thing before me will not give me that opportunity.

The creature steps over the corpse of the she-wolf and glances at it, sniffing the air. Then it stares at me and smiles. "Yowa has abandoned you, Cub. She has granted you to me. The spirit of Wendigo is not a curse but a blessing."

It lifts its foot to take another step, and the she-wolf's jaws open and snap shut around its ankle. The creature screams and stomps the ribs of the wolf, but it refuses to let go.

I step forward slowly and hold my knife in front of me to help the wolf-mother fight the beast. But instead of helping, I pitch to my knees and spit up blood, losing the knife in the fall. As I search for the blade, I see the eyes again. Bright and red. Larger than before. Flanked by four other pairs—smaller and farther away, but just as bright.

"Good-bye, Father," I whisper. "I will wait for you in the land of the spirits of my ancestors."

The eyes emerge from the shelter of the trees, and I behold the tallest creature I've ever seen. Taller than me sitting on my father's shoulders and as wide as the base of the greatest pine in the forest. It stinks of dirty fur and stands slightly slumped over, its arms resting limply at its sides, not quite reaching its knees.

I bow my head and fall to the ground.

It stands quietly facing me while four others like it come into the clearing and stand beside it.

The thing held by the she-wolf stops fighting. "No, you can't have him. He's mine," it hisses.

The largest of the hairy men walks forward and stands over me. Then it kneels and sniffs my chest.

The loathsome creature possessed by Wendigo tears itself free from the wolf's jaws and leaps at the great beast-man over me.

My strength gives out, and I let darkness consume me.

Rain falls on my skin, cold and heavy, and I open my eyes.

The clearing is empty, aside from myself and the remains of the wolf-mother.

Her body has been skinned and is held above a fire by a tent of branches. The fire burns low, and I can tell I have been asleep a long time. The meat is cooked and calls to my hungry gut.

My lacerated gut.

I reach to feel the wounds and find them covered. The she-wolf's skin has been wrapped around me and tied together with long grass woven into a fine thin rope. I hurt all over, and it will be a long time before I can walk without pain, but I am alive.

And Yowa has made me a man unlike anyone else of the Aniyunwiya people. She has blessed me with the mightiest scar of my tribe. She has given me the living memory of both the Tsul Kalu of the mountain and the Wendigo from the north.

And I know my purpose of my quest.

My people will not fall into disbelief, even with the coming of the white man. My scar will remind me, and it will remind them. And one day, when I am old like Gentle Bear, the boys will come to me, and I will tell them the story over again as they go into the forest to become men themselves. And my words will go with them and be law and be all they have in that day.

So I eat. I will need the strength to return home and to tell my father and Gentle Bear and the others my new name: Wolf Who Remembers.

Yalobusha County, 1862

Ken Teutsch

It's simple enough, I suppose, how it happened—how the boy from Iowa came to be in Mississippi. Mr. Lincoln wanted Vicksburg and sent General Grant to take it. In the spring of that year, General Grant led his men into a meat grinder that they named after a church: Shiloh. Twenty thousand casualties in two days. In purely practical terms, this created a need for a lot of new soldiers down in Mississippi, and so William Allen came south.

As I say. Simple. Great people make decisions, and little people pay the consequences.

So here was Pvt. Willie Allen at the end of a dreary day, on the seat of a wagon drawn by two U.S. Army mules. Next to him on the seat was a great hulking man from Chicago named Kretzinger. Corporal Kretzinger. Willie Allen had only just got off the train in Memphis and marched down, but this Kretzinger was an older man, a grey and grizzled man, a veteran. He had been through the meat grinder. Willie was the kind of fellow who tried to get along with everyone, but he pretty quickly gave up trying to be friendly with Kretzinger. Kretzinger was German, a city man with no patience for little green replacements like this country boy from Iowa. He was big and constantly snarling, forever ill-humored for no reason Willie could see. By now, Willie just wanted to stay as far away as he could, but that wasn't far on a wagon seat.

To make matters worse, Kretzinger had on his knee a crockery jug he had picked up a couple of houses back, and he was working as fast as he could at emptying it. As the level in the jug got lower and lower, Willie squeezed farther and farther over on the seat until he was in danger of toppling off.

The wagon they were driving was loaded with corn and meal and flour, sacks of potatoes, baskets of peas and beans, buckets of molasses—all kinds of foodstuffs. And despite everything they had told Willie about the rules of war, he couldn't quite shake the feeling that it was all stolen.

The reason for this was that shortly after Willie got to Memphis on the train—they'd been drilling in Illinois, then taken to Columbus, Kentucky, and from there down to Tennessee—Forrest and Van Dorn, rebel generals, came west with cavalry and started harassing the Union troops, tearing up the railroad tracks, upsetting the supply lines and communications, capturing supply depots, and sowing confusion all through the rearguard of the Union army. This was calculated to disrupt the offensive, of course, and to some extent, it did. But Gen. Ulysses S. Grant was nothing if not innovative. He had an idea that would serve two purposes. It would feed his army, and it would teach a lesson to people who rise up against their government. He issued an order. The order was to send out troops to fifteen miles on either side of the road between Holly Springs and Grenada, Mississippi, to gather up everything edible. That's how he would feed his army. When the local people came to General Grant in dismay about this, he shrugged and said, "You cannot expect armed men to starve in the midst of plenty." So instead of marching into battle against Johnny Reb, as he thought he was coming down here to do, Willie Allen had been spending his days prying sacks of potatoes out of the hands of weeping women.

It was mostly women because the men had gone for soldiers or were in hiding, afraid of being taken for soldiers. The order supposedly said that they were to leave enough food for the people to get by for a month or so, but that part of the order tended to be overlooked. Day in and day out now since he had gotten to Mississippi, they'd been going out in teams and rounding up the hogs and cattle, raiding root cellars and pantries, and plundering barns, corn cribs, and henhouses.

He had signed on to be a hero, and they had made him a chicken thief.

It was even a little hard sometimes for Willie to remember that these people were the enemy. He kept looking into the eyes of these women and seeing his mother's eyes, and he kept seeing his own face in the dirty little faces peering around from behind the skirts. But you have to be hard to be a soldier. That's the way it has always been. He would remind himself, thinking, *They're rebels. They're only getting what's coming to them.*

But now, on this particular day, as he was trying to slide away from Corporal Kretzinger on the bench, they were heading back to camp. The rest of the squad had gone on earlier, driving the livestock. It was getting dark. It got dark early now; it was more than half a year after Shiloh. The last week or so, the weather had turned wetter and colder, and now the wind kicked up out of the north to make it worse. It was getting dark, and it was darker still because it was coming on to rain again. They were passing back by a house that they had already hit that morning. It was a low log house, not much more than a shack, really. This wasn't the rich land near the river. There were no big houses, no fields of cotton, no gangs of slaves. Just hardscrabble people. As the wagon rolled up to the front of the house, Kretzinger mumbled something. Willie didn't understand him.

"What's that?" he said.

"Stop and marm mum . . ."

"Uh . . . all right."

33

Kretzinger wanted to stop at the house to warm up.

As the mules shuffled to a stop and the wheels creaked, Willie saw the door of the house swing open. A shape appeared in the doorway. A woman. Willie hadn't gone inside the house earlier, so he hadn't really seen this woman when they came through the first time. He saw her silhouetted now against the glow of a lamp inside. She stood watching for a moment, then slammed the door. Kretzinger set the brake and got down. He ignored Willie, tucked his jug under his arm, and started toward the house.

Willie didn't want to go in the house, but he couldn't just sit out there and wait for the rain, so he grabbed his rifle and climbed down. He sometimes felt foolish with that rifle, given the duty he'd been at lately. Still, you never knew what was going to happen, and they had told him to keep his bayonet fixed as some of these people had vicious dogs. By the time he got down, Kretzinger had already reached the cabin door. He made no pretense of asking permission. He just shoved at the door with the heel of his hand, and when it didn't give, he took a step back and slammed into it with his shoulder. The little latch or whatever held it shut popped right off and Kretzinger walked inside. Willie followed after.

The first thing Willie thought when he stepped through the door was *That sure smells good*. He looked around the room. There was a lamp on the table against the far wall. A door led to a room off to the left. He could see part of a bedstead in there in the shaft of lamplight. Those two rooms made up the whole house. There was not much furniture in the room. Not much of anything. Next to the bedroom door was a low table with a large book on it, and Willie knew right away that it was the family Bible because there was one just like it in his own house. Big book with pages in it to write down all the births and the deaths. And there was the woman. She was standing in the middle of the room on a square horse blanket thrown down on the floor for a rug.

She had on a blue dress, faded from age and many washings. He wasn't sure how old she was. A farm woman. Lines on her face from work and from care. Dark hair pulled up. She had high cheekbones like maybe there was some Indian blood in her family. And dark eyes. *Black* eyes. Those eyes were burning, looking at these two soldiers as they walked into her home.

Now Willie realized what the smell was. There was a low iron stove near the far wall, and on the stove was a skillet with biscuits in it. For a second, he couldn't quite think why this seemed peculiar, and then he remembered. She shouldn't have any flour to make biscuits. They had cleaned her out. Willie looked at Kretzinger and saw that he was thinking the same thing. The big man carefully set his jug down on the table by the lamp, put his hands on his hips, narrowed his eyes, and said, "What's this now?"

The woman didn't say anything.

Kretzinger turned and looked at Willie. "You see that?" he said.

It sounded like "You zee zat?" When Kretzinger drank, he talked more like a German. Willie nodded. Kretzinger turned back to the woman. "That's a nice trick," he said.

Kretzinger started walking toward her. "Holding out," he said. The woman tensed as he drew nearer, but she didn't move. "How? How did you . . ." He stopped. He got a quizzical look on his face. He looked down at the rug. The woman's face tightened up even more, but she didn't take her eyes off Kretzinger.

The big man looked back at Willie, and his face creased and crackled into a smile. "Smart!" he said, and he put a long finger alongside his nose. He stood up straight and lifted one foot off the floor as though about to go into a dance. *Thump, thump, thump* went his boot heel. He turned his unpleasant smile back on the woman.

"Pretty smart, you rebs, is it?" he said.

He stepped back, reached down, and grabbed a corner of the horse blanket and flipped it back. There, beneath it, was a trap door. There was a cellar under the kitchen floor, and they had somehow completely missed it earlier. Kretzinger stood back up and started laughing. "Pretty good!" he barked, and he looked at Willie again. "Pretty good, hah?"

The woman suddenly came unfrozen. Her hands went up to the front of her dress and clasped just below her chin. She started shaking her head. Words came pouring out now, in that drawly way they talked down here. Her voice was partly both pleading and partly reasoning. "Mister," she said, "there ain't nothing down there. It's just some preserves is all. You took my hogs and you took my cow. It's dead winter comin' on, and I gotta live somehow. I done give you everything—everything *big*."

Her pleading was pathetic and would have moved a lot of people. But Kretzinger didn't give a damn about that woman. It was partly the liquor, but nowhere near all, for the fact was Kretzinger didn't give a damn about any rebel. As for plead- ing—he had heard a lot of pleading lately. There was a lot of pleading at Shiloh. "Give me water. Don't let me die." Pleading didn't help *them* any, did it? Didn't help his friend Walt or his cousin Franz there in the Hornet's Nest. And this bitch's son or husband might have been the one as pulled the trigger.

Willie hadn't seen and heard the things Kretzinger had seen and heard. Would he have acted differently if he had? No way to know. All we can say is that what he did do was to step for- ward and speak. "Corporal Kretzinger!" The big man turned his hard face toward him, and Willie took half a step back again. "We have these biscuits. Why don't we just take these biscuits for our supper?" Kretzinger said nothing. The woman looked at young Willie and held her breath. "Wagon's full anyway," the boy went on. "Why don't we just—"

Kretzinger snapped at him. "Shut up! We got orders, don't we? We take it all." Willie knew those weren't quite the orders and that Kretzinger wasn't usually such a stickler for orders. And he almost said so. But he didn't. "We take it all!" Kretzinger repeated, and he made a gesture like cutting with a sword. He turned his glare back on the woman. "I want what's in the *keller.*" She just looked at him and didn't move. He pushed her, and she staggered back against the wall.

She cried out now, the reasoning tone gone from her voice. "No! Don't you go down there!" Kretzinger reached down and grabbed the handle and started to pull up the trapdoor. Willie saw the woman look from Kretzinger to the stove. Before he could move—before he could even blink—she had grabbed the skillet and swung it at Kretzinger's head.

He saw it coming out of the corner of his eye and tried to duck it, which saved him. Instead of on the skull, he took the blow on his shoulder. The biscuits flew into the air in all directions. Kretzinger dropped the trapdoor, stood up, and gave an animal howl of pain; he turned to the woman and hit her as hard as he could. She crashed into the wall and fell to the floor. Kretzinger kept yowling and rubbing his shoulder, cussing in German. Then he reached again for the trapdoor.

Amazingly, the woman got up. She still held the skillet, and Willie, frozen, could only think, *Hot! That must be hot!* The woman started toward Kretzinger again.

The sudden violence, the noise, hitting the woman—it all shocked Willie so that he couldn't move. He couldn't believe the woman had gotten back up. He couldn't believe this was happening. Kretzinger spun toward him, and—just like that, like a magic trick—his rifle was gone. One second, Willie was holding it, and then it was gone and Kretzinger had it. Kretzinger turned back toward the advancing woman and stuck the bayonet right into her. Then he pulled it out. Willie couldn't speak, couldn't shout. Kretzinger stabbed the woman again. Pulled it out again. The woman fell to the floor, stretched across the trapdoor.

Kretzinger stabbed her again.

Willie felt like he'd been dropped into icy water. He heard a voice yelling, and it must have been his own. "What did you do? What did you do?" Kretzinger wheeled around to face him, and Willie Allen thought, *I'm going to die now. He'll do it to me too.*

But Kretzinger didn't kill him. He swung his arm wide and slapped Willie down. "Shut up! Stop that hollering!" And everything got quiet. The cold wind moved around the corners of the house. Something popped in the stove. Kretzinger stood still a long moment, rubbing his shoulder, his eyes jammed closed in pain. He growled something in German. Finally, he turned and looked at the woman, and Willie followed his gaze. They both stared at her and at the blood—so much blood— coming out and spreading across the floor.

As the blinding rage oozed out of him, Kretzinger began to realize that this was bad. A rebel, yes, but a civilian and a woman. This could be trouble. Big trouble. He started cussing. He cussed the woman and he cussed Willie Allen. He turned away from the bloody form and threw the rifle down on the floor. He stepped over, dragged the woman over to one side, and sat her up.

When Kretzinger lifted the woman up, she looked at Willie. Or that is, Willie could see her face, and she seemed to be looking at him. Those black, black eyes. They were dead now, and they were looking straight at him and straight through him. Kretzinger jerked open the trapdoor and shoved the woman. She pitched forward, vanishing into the black hole below—and *boom*—the trapdoor fell shut.

Kretzinger stalked over to Willie. "Now listen to me, you pup," he said. "Eh? You listening? Ain't just one man will hang for this. If anybody hangs, it's *both* of us! You hear? You say a word, you go down too, boy. Eh? Whose knife was it stabbed her? Huh?"

Willie couldn't say anything. Kretzinger began to pace back and forth. He tracked through the blood. He groaned from the pain in his shoulder and a new pain growing in his head. There was a sick panic in his darting eyes. "Look here," he said finally. "We're going back. We go on back tonight. But I gotta rest a minute. I gotta rest." He looked past Willie into the other room. "Look at that! That's a featherbed in that room there! I ain't even *seen* a featherbed in a *year*!" He gave a humorless bark of laughter. "Little rest here. And then we leave."

He walked into the bedroom and slapped the door closed behind him, leaving Willie sitting there in this room, the lamp flickering on the table and the pool of blood on the floor. There was a creaking of the bed, and Kretzinger groaned, and then there was nothing. Just the wind picking up outside.

It was as though Willie was in a trance. Time oozed around and past him. His shoulder was against the table with the Bible on it, and thinking of the Bible made him think of his mother. How she cried when he left home and how he laughed and told her he'd be all right and that the Union needed him. He didn't know how much time passed. He was unaware of anything until he heard a new sound. A steady *drip, drip, drip*—the blood falling through the cracks in the floor and down into the cellar. More time passed, and Willie's mind went blank until another sound came. Something tapped the walls and pattered on the roof. It had begun to rain. He realized that beneath the muttering of the world outside, he could hear a voice—a low, raspy voice—his own.

He heard himself saying over and over, "I'm sorry. I'm sorry. I'm sorry." He was talking to that woman down in the cellar, and he was talking to his mother back in Iowa. When he tried to see his mother in his mind, she had that woman's eyes.

"I'm sorry. I'm sorry. I'm—" A rustle. A scratch.

It came from under that trapdoor.

Willie's mind spun loose for a few seconds, and he held his breath, listening. *Oh, dear Jesus,* he thought, *there's rats down there!* Rats down there—and that woman, *she* was down there! And those eyes. All he could see were those eyes, and he knew those eyes were still open. *And there's rats down there.* His breath ripped loose with a tearing sound. Now he couldn't seem to get enough air.

But then there was a thump, and wait a minute now.

That wasn't any rat.

Willie tried to push himself up the wall, but his feet just skittered on the floor. He looked around at the closed bedroom door. He heard Kretzinger's raspy breathing, a half-snore. He looked back toward the center of the room. The lamp cast its light on the wall and the ceiling, but the trapdoor lay in the table's black shadow. The noises continued. A scratching. A rustle. Another thump. A creak.

The trapdoor was opening.

It was like one of those dreams where he tried to stir but his limbs wouldn't obey. He watched the door swing up higher,

higher, and then fall with a muffled thud onto the rolled up horse blanket behind it. He saw a shape in the shadow coming up out of the hole, swaying slightly as it rose up into the light.

And there she was.

The blood looked black in the lamplight. Blood was streaked all over the faded blue gingham. Her hair had fallen down. It was wild, and it swirled all around her face. But he could see the eyes. The eyes—unchanged, dark, black—looking straight at him, into him. She stepped toward him, sending her shadow across the floor and up the wall, until she stood over him. He drew in a long shaking breath.

"I'm sorry," he said again. "I'm sorry."

She leaned toward him, and Willie gave a small involuntary whimper. But she wasn't leaning down for him. She straightened up again, holding his rifle. He had forgotten that it was there on the floor.

The edge of her dress brushed across him, the wetness cold on his face. She pushed open the door to the bedroom. Kretzinger's snoring got louder, but it was no louder than the sigh of the wind and patter of the rain. There was a pause long enough for Willie to begin to hope that he really had been dreaming. Yes, dreaming. A sort of relief began to grow in him. Then came a sharp tearing sound, and Kretzinger's soft snore staggered, stumbled, and twisted into a cry. There was a rush of noise as Kretzinger thrashed among the bedclothes.

The rifle went off like thunder, and Willie was on his feet.

He didn't remember opening the door or leaving the house. He found himself in the rain, running. He ran past the wagon and the U.S. Army mules. He didn't think of where he was running to. He didn't think of anything at all. He just ran. Across the lane, into the blackness among the trees. Just running and stumbling, arms raised to shield his face, falling and rising to keep on running. Behind him, the house was quiet.

Willie's mother back in Iowa never saw her oldest boy again. He was a Plains boy, after all. Even in his right mind, he would have been bewildered by those woods and sloughs, creeks and thickets of northern Mississippi. Even natives sometimes lost themselves in that country and were never seen again. "Hogs got him" is what the locals would say. William Allen ran into the woods, and that was that.

The next morning, some people came, neighbors passing along down the track. Everybody was on the move. All the people in the country were packing up what little they had left. Winter was here, and they had nothing to eat. The lucky ones had kinfolks in Alabama or someplace where the Yankees hadn't gone yet. The rest didn't know where they were going or what they would eat tomorrow. People came by the house not long after daylight, and they stopped and they said, "Look at this!"

There was a Yankee army wagon in front of the house. Those poor mules still stood there in harness as they had all night. The door of the house stood wide open. People stopped, and they gathered, looked at the strangely troubling open door, and wondered what to do. Someone hailed the house. No one answered.

They got up their nerve, and they went up and looked in the door. They saw the blood. They saw what was in the bed. And they saw someone sitting there on the floor. Sitting there looking down through the trapdoor into the cellar hole.

A woman eased up to the figure on the floor, reached out, and touched her shoulder. "Sarah? Sarah girl! What happened? Where's your mama? Sarah? Where's your mama at, girl?"

Sarah didn't answer. She just stared into the hole.

Some things never change. Great people make decisions. Little people pay the consequences.

Yankees in Georgia: Chasing Ghosts and the General along the Old W&A Railroad

Lewis Powell IV

Oh dear, Yankees in Georgia! How did they ever get in?
—Aunt Pittypat in the 1939 film Gone with the Wind

As you approach the General today, it almost feels like a living thing. Strategically placed speakers provide all the sounds a working engine would make. With its bright paint and polished brass, the massive locomotive hardly seems old, but it's an iron horse that has seen a whirlwind of history in its 150 years.

As the General began chugging out of Atlanta's Union Station at 4:00 am on April 12, 1862, toward Chattanooga, no one knew that this obscure locomotive was taking a ride into history and legend. That very day, the war had been going on for exactly a year, almost to the hour. A year earlier, the bombardment on Fort Sumter, a Union stronghold at the mouth of Charleston Harbor, had begun with a Confederate victory after nearly two days of shelling. The city of Atlanta, waking from its slumber, was too distracted by its morning bustle to notice the little engine's departure.

That morning in 1862, as the General began making its way north with passengers and freight, a group of Yankees, selected from a variety of Ohio infantry companies, and two civilians began rising in their Marietta hotel, the Fletcher House, located next to the tracks just off the town square. Oddly, this group of soldiers on a military sortie was headed by a civilian: the mysterious (at least to historians) James J. Andrews of Kentucky. The motley group of soldiers, who had traveled in small groups into enemy territory in disguise, met in Andrews' room to lay forth plans for the raid that was to take place in the next few hours. After dismissing the doubts of one of the higher-ranking soldiers in the group, Andrews concluded his orders by adamantly stating, "I will accomplish my purpose or leave my bones to bleach in Dixie." With that benediction, the group boarded their train.

Marietta, once a small town some miles north of Atlanta, has now been caught in the fingers of Atlanta's sprawl. The farms and plantations that existed between the cities have been replaced by highways and strip malls, though parts of Marietta's town square still appear as James Andrews and his men would have seen it. This includes the massive Fletcher House, later called the Kennesaw House and now the home of the Marietta Museum of History. As well as housing artifacts, the old hotel also houses spirits, possibly in the hundreds.

The room where Andrews defined the day's mission has been recreated, though the building has seen sweeping changes since its early days as a hotel. As with so many Georgia cities along the railroad, Marietta saw an influx of wounded Confederates as the war progressed. The Fletcher House was pressed into service as a hospital, and its halls and rooms that once rang with giggles of delight were filled with moans of pain and death. Following the war, the building resumed service as a hotel and has had a variety of uses over its history, but it is perhaps its wartime usage that resonates down into the twenty-first century.

Staff and visitors have had a variety of odd experiences within the halls of this hallowed edifice. Author Barbara Duffey, while attempting to photograph the building from the outside, remarked that she felt the "presence of many forces." Later, when she began to glance around the second floor, she briefly was greeted by the scene of a Civil War–era surgery overseen by a bloody doctor standing over a patient. A male spirit, possibly the same doctor, has been spotted in the building as well. Even more amazing is a photograph taken by the museum's director in 2003. He was shocked to see anomalies appear on the screen from a security camera. Grabbing his camera, he snapped a photo of the screen showing the stark white silhouette of a woman wearing period clothing. Some even speculate that James Andrews may be among the spirits walking the halls here, where he spent his last night in comfort.

After getting their orders for the mission, the group of twenty-one (two had not been awakened, having failed to pay the porter) left the comforts of the Fletcher House for the chilly train platform next door. The group spread out so as to not arouse the suspicion of other travelers. The General pulled in at 5:00 am, and the raiders boarded for their trip into history and, for some, oblivion.

Spread out among the passenger cars, this group quietly rode until their first stop.

An hour later, the call was heard. "Big Shanty! Twenty minutes for breakfast."

The sun was rising upon Big Shanty, a diminutive settlement that consisted mostly of a depot and the large wood-frame two-story Lacy Hotel, which fronted the railroad. Across the tracks, the Confederate government had set up Camp McDonald for training new recruits. In a field of neat white tents, some seven thousand new Confederate troops were just getting up for a new day. Though armed only with pikes, the scene surely presented a jolt to the raiders, who were preparing to steal a locomotive right out from under their very noses.

Much to the relief of the Yankees, the train's entire crew and all of its passengers disembarked for the warmth and hospitality of the Lacy Hotel. With an air of nonchalance, Andrews and his two railroad engineers climbed into the General's cab and signaled to the others to take their places. The passenger cars were unhooked quietly, and the rest of the men boarded the three empty boxcars just behind the locomotive. The engine's steam was raised, and within moments, they were off. From his table inside the Lacy Hotel, Conductor William Fuller spied the locomotive as it began to chug away from the station. Jumping up from the table, Fuller and two of his men began to run in pursuit of the escaped engine.

Standing in the shadow of Kennesaw Mountain, Big Shanty, now known as Kennesaw, sprawls leisurely along the I-75 corridor, which roughly parallels the old Western & Atlantic Railroad. The Lacy Hotel was burned by Sherman as he marched on Atlanta in 1864, while the depot has been replaced by a more modern building. However, the railroad tracks follow much the same course that they did in 1862. The theft of the General would not be the last major event here during this war.

As General Sherman began to cut a swath toward Atlanta in June of 1864, he was faced with heavy Confederate fortifications on Kennesaw Mountain. Sherman was forced to attack the Confederates head on, and he lost the battle with heavy casualties of nearly three thousand compared to the Confederates' one thousand casualties. Though this defeat did not quell Sherman's relentless drive toward Atlanta, it did delay capture of the city and put Kennesaw on the map. The landscape around the mountain was left strewn with bodies, equipment, and spirits. The more important sections of the battlefield have been preserved, but other sections have been lost to Atlanta's relentless progress. Some of the hallowed ground now sits under shopping malls, convenience stores, and housing developments, many of which are haunted as a result. One particular subdivision has had so much activity it was featured on television's *Unsolved Mysteries*.

Visitors to terrain preserved by Kennesaw Mountain National Battlefield Park have also had experiences with apparitions of those killed here. Some modern roads now crisscross the old farm fields that saw action, and it was along one of these roads a few years ago that a father and his son had an unusual experience. Late one evening, this pair was startled to see a figure on horseback dart in front of their car. The father slowed the car down, and they watched the figure, which they identified as a Union cavalry officer, as he crossed the road and right through a split rail fence on the opposite side before disappearing in the looming darkness.

The locomotive, now under Yankee control, sped away from Big Shanty with Conductor Fuller and two other men doggedly pursuing on foot. The Yankees paused briefly at Moon's Station, not far from Big Shanty, and "borrowed" a claw bar from the work crew there. They proceeded at the usual speed of sixteen miles per hour and stopped again to check the engine and cut the telegraph wire. The train arrived in Acworth to the confusion of the passengers and crew waiting on the platform. It stopped only momentarily and then headed on toward the small village of Allatoona.

Allatoona Pass is very quiet today. Little remains of the town after most of it disappeared under the Lake Allatoona reservoir. The building of the reservoir led to the rerouting of the railroad, so now the only chugging in the pass comes from joggers or hikers, short of breath after climbing to see the remains of the earthen star forts that were built to protect this vital pass. Three forts were constructed: one on either side of the cut with a bridge between them and a larger fort overlooking the Etowah River. It was here that on October 5, 1864, after Atlanta's fall, Confederate forces attacked the well-fortified pass. However, the attack was unsuccessful, and the Union soldiers retained control.

A few days after this action, a coffin arrived at the Allatoona depot. Inside was the body of a young Confederate soldier, though there was nothing else to identify the corpse. Some ladies of the town saw to it that the soldier was buried along the tracks just north of the pass under a stone that read An Unknown Hero. As trains continued to use the pass, crews and passengers reported seeing a young Confederate soldier running along the track near the lone grave. In the 1940s, when the tracks were rerouted due to the construction of Lake Allatoona, the grave was moved as well. The pass has since remained silent. Considered one of the most undisturbed battlefields in the country, the Allatoona Pass battlefield is now visited by tourists and the occasional spirit.

The Confederates, still chasing the General on foot, reached Moon's Station, where the Yankees had borrowed the claw bar. After finding that the raiders had left some thirty minutes prior, the trio took a handcar. The trio dodged obstacles and missing rails in their pursuit before they were thrown off the line just north of the Allatoona Pass by a missing rail. Just across the Etowah River Bridge, a target that had not been destroyed by the raiders, Fuller and his men spotted the engine Yonah with a full head of steam at work at the Cooper's Iron Works spur.

Andrews and his men had the chance to destroy the Yonah as they passed the spur, though in doing so, they would have attracted the attention of the employees working there. Instead, they passed quietly by, but they were not unnoticed. When Fuller arrived sometime later, the men were still confused by the earlier passage of the General with no passengers. Everything made sense when they were informed of the situation. The Yonah was hooked up to a flatcar with crossties, rails, and tools and sent north after its stolen sibling.

The Yankees left behind more astonished passengers as they passed the Cartersville depot and headed toward lonely Cass Station. Stopping at Cass Station to load up on wood and water, Andrews blithely plied the stationmaster with a tale of taking an emergency load of gunpowder north. With information on the recent Confederate defeats at Shiloh and Huntsville, the stationmaster believed the story, and the raiders continued toward Kingston, the largest rail yard between Atlanta and Chattanooga.

Now just a quiet small town, Kingston was a busy spot before and during the Civil War. Four large railroad sidings here allowed for trains to pass in opposite directions while the main line also met the spur to Rome, a city in West Georgia. It was here that Andrews had to be especially slick in dealing with the station employees and switchmen as well as other train conductors. Again, he spouted his tale of being an emergency gunpowder train. He was believed, though some did wonder why no corroboration came over the telegraph lines from the south. The General was directed to a siding while two trains from Chattanooga passed, and the locomotive resumed its northerly course with nary a soul in Kingston suspecting the boxcars were loaded with armed Yankees.

The Yonah pulled into Kingston a short while later, and Fuller took the speedier William R. Smith to continue the chase. The General had stopped just outside of Kingston to construct a barricade across the tracks and lifted another rail. But Andrews worried about keeping to the schedule to avoid unnecessary suspicion. After stopping again to cut the telegraph wires and obstruct the line, the General hurried forward, reaching speeds of nearly sixty miles per hour as the crew began burning oil in the locomotive's firebox. They stopped in Adairsville and told the same lie about gunpowder before continuing toward Calhoun, where the racing train nearly collided with a train pulled by the Catoosa. After an angry encounter with the Catoosa's crew, the raiders headed north, hoping to reach Chattanooga in good time.

The William R. Smith was slowed by the obstructions on the line but still made good time toward Adairsville. Two miles south of the city, it met the powerful southbound Texas, pulling a number of passenger cars. After relating to the conductor what had happened, the Texas was backed two miles to Adairsville. The passenger cars were put on a siding, but the engine could not be turned around. It was decided that the powerful engine could pursue the General just as fast backward as forward. The chase was on!

Just north of Calhoun, Andrews and his men paused again to cut the telegraph wires and lift another rail. As they worked, they were surprised to hear a train whistle approaching. The Texas came chugging around the bend backward. The men dropped the rail and boarded the stolen train. The General had not stopped again for fuel or water since Cass Station and was running low. A boxcar was quickly unhooked and left on the track to block the oncoming Texas, but after creeping over the loosened rail, the Texas was able to just hook up the loose boxcar and continue the chase.

The Yankee raiders in the final boxcar broke through the back wall and began tossing crossties onto the track. Unfortunately, given the speed of the train, many of these bounced off the rails. The second boxcar was also dropped, but again, it was coupled to the Texas, and the chase continued toward the covered Oostanaula River Bridge, another of the main targets of the raid. The bridge, soaked by days of rain, was too wet to set ablaze. Both engines sped north with the Yankees increasingly nervous about their pursuers. The General pulled into the small hamlet of Tilton, where it stopped briefly to load some wood in the tender and water into the engine, but with the Texas in hot pursuit, they were only able to load a small amount.

As the General sped through the rail yard at Dalton, the stunned telegrapher there notified Confederate authorities in Chattanooga of the situation. General Leadbetter quickly dispatched a train with soldiers south to create an ambush at Chickamauga. The chase led through the hamlet of Tunnel Hill, just south of the lengthy railroad tunnel through Chetoogeta Mountain. The General shot through the brick and limestone tunnel, leaving only smoke in its wake.

Completed just a few years before, this engineering marvel was among the first railroad tunnels in the United States. Skirmishes were fought here later in the war with soldiers on both sides attempting to destroy the tunnel, though the act was never carried out. It served for decades until a larger modern tunnel was constructed in the 1920s right next to it. After being abandoned by the Central of Georgia Railway (which took over the W&A line after the war), the tunnel became a curiosity to local kids who would dare each other to walk the length of the dark and gloomy passage. A proposal to seal the tunnel brought local history buffs to the rescue. The tunnel has been restored, and the battlefield adjacent to it is being preserved. Visitors can now take tours through the long and cold tunnel, where spirits still roam. Locals tell of mysterious campfires on the mountain around the tunnel, while some still detect the smell of death in the area.

The Texas approached the tunnel with apprehension, fearing that the raiders may have left obstructions in the gloom. However, the Yankees were fleeing with such speed that nothing was done. The Texas passed through safely and picked up speed again. After passing through Ringgold, the weary crew on the General had exhausted their wood and was now throwing anything flammable into the firebox, including Andrews' saddlebags. Around 12:30 pm, the General approached an uphill grade, and the engine ran out of steam. Andrews and his men scattered into the mountainous alien country exhausted, hungry, and defeated.

Word spread to farms and villages throughout the region that train thieves were on the loose. Locals charged into the mountains to find the "damn Yankees" and bring them to justice. Within days, all the raiders were in chains, and they were soon transferred to Chattanooga to stand trial. The raiders were incarcerated in an infamous hellhole called Swims Jail. The jail held prisoners on its sealed ground floor, which was accessible only by a trapdoor. In this squalid hole, all twenty-three raiders (the two who had overslept were also caught) were kept until trial. The Yankees stewed until May, when they were transported to Atlanta for trial on a train pulled by none other than the General.

Though the jail itself was torn down years ago, the site at the corner of Fifth and Lookout Streets still retains an air of negative energy. One ghost-tour guide has recorded a number of remarkable experiences at the site. Shadow figures have been seen darting about, and photographs taken in the area reveal orbs.

After quick trials, the raiders were found guilty and sentenced to death by hanging. As the leader, James Andrews was the first to be executed. He was taken to the Atlanta Graveyard and paraded before his hastily dug grave before stepping onto the gallows. When the platform dropped, the rope was too long, and his feet barely touched the ground while he strangled to death at the end of his rope. More than a week later, the Confederate authorities loaded seven more Yankees onto a cart bound for the same gallows. With a noose around his neck, George Wilson, an Ohio shoemaker, pleaded the group's innocence, stating that they were only doing their duty as soldiers. His pleas went unheeded. The platform dropped and five necks broke; two of the ropes snapped, and the condemned were properly hanged an hour later. All their bodies were interred near the site. But with those eight deaths, the executions ended. Some of the remaining raiders had escaped, and the rest did not face the gallows.

The Atlanta Graveyard, now called Oakland Cemetery, swelled with Confederate dead during the war. Its heart, rank upon rank of simple stones, is haunted by those who eternally sleep there. Shadowy figures have been spotted among the graves, quite possibly the spirits of the eight men who were executed here. Near the huge stone lion representing the dying Confederacy, some have heard a voice intoning the names of the dead—an eternal roll call. However, the raiders no longer lie here. Their bodies were returned to Chattanooga, where they were buried at the National Cemetery.

Under a monument topped with their prize—a marble statue of the General—Andrews and seven of his men sleep. Legend tells that during a full moon, the marble train leaves its position and chugs through the cemetery. The actual General, after many trips around the country, now resides in the Southern

Museum of Civil War and Locomotive History in Kennesaw. The building, next to the modern CSX railroad tracks, is located just yards from where the engine began its ride into legend. Museum staff have reported that even now, 150 years later, the shades of the raiders still linger about the engine, recalling the Great Locomotive Chase.

A Hunnerd Dollars, Gold

Peter Mehren

When I heard the new recruits being taught how to do the Rebel Yell, I was truly frightened. How quickly they all joined in and how enthusiastic and savage—prehuman—it sounded. I was reminded of what the Duke of Wellington said when one of his officers asked if he thought the rough British soldiers at Waterloo would frighten Napoleon and his troops—'I do not know what they'll do to the enemy, but by God, they frighten me!'

"And I knew that as the wealthy son of an even wealthier planter, I'd be made an officer . . . and I knew that I lack the character to control them. I'm not leadership material. At which point, the agent selling substitutes set up his table with you and the others seated on the ground around him. I bought my way out by purchasing your services for a hundred dollars, five twenty-dollar United States of America gold pieces."

"He only gave me four, sir."

"That seems an excessive commission, 20 percent."

"And worse than that, sir, when he sent it to my wife, she got only sixty. And the bank in our village charged her ten more to change it to Confederate dollars. So the way I figure it, sir, you owe her fifty dollars, Confederate or Yankee, sir, for my having died instead of you, sir."

"And that's why you're haunting me?"

"It seems so, sir. That and burying me properly, sir."

"But you know we're on our way to California right now, don't you? Hundreds of miles from Alabama."

"You may be, sir. But I'm just with you, wherever you are. I know nothing else, sir—where we are, how we got here, why or how I found you, why I can't leave you, sir."

That night, while dining alone, Swain was approached by an attractive but slightly used lady. He invited her to join him for a nightcap. She wanted champagne but agreed to settle for a simple red wine. After which, of course, they retired to Swain's room in the hotel, the desk clerk smiling at the dollar Swain put on his counter before he and his lady of the night ascended.

But only a few minutes later, she screamed in terror and pushed Swain off. "What's that!" she shouted as she leapt from the bed and ran, naked, to the door and out into the hall.

Swain had glanced over his shoulder to see whatever she was pointing at and had glimpsed, ere it faded, a floating face between him and the room's ceiling, with wide-open eyes, pulled-back lips, and an evil look somewhere between a smile and a snarl. And then it, like the female, was gone.

"Did you do that?" Swain said.

Faintly, he heard, "Yes, sir."

"Why?"

"Be alert, sir. Why I know things, I do not understand. But in a moment, your door would have been broken open by a huge and nasty man, claiming to be her husband and robbing you of all your possessions at gunpoint."

"Am I safe now?"

"I would urge you to return to the lobby after packing whatever you've taken out of your portmanteau, sir, and spend the night there, perhaps with the pistol from your suitcase held instead in a coat pocket for ease of use, sir."

And so Swain spent the night seated, drinking coffee and fighting sleep. He could rest in the stagecoach as he continued his westward journey.

But as Swain and his ghostly fellow traveler crossed Texas, he was again warned. The voice spoke to him as he entered a wayside hotel restaurant. "Sir, try to be inconspicuous. Do not engage in conversation with anyone, I urge you."

Nonetheless, as he sat alone, eating, two rough men approached him. One said, "You look mighty fancy. You're not from here, are you?"

Swain smiled slightly and shook his head.

"Nothing to say?"

"Just passing through." And he heard a sigh.

"That accent—you're a Southerner, aren't you?"

Swain nodded in the affirmative, almost imperceptibly.

"Why aren't you in the army?"

"I'm not mad at anyone. That's why I'm heading west."

"Well, I'm mad at you." And the pair took another step toward Swain . . . at which point, the wine bottle on Swain's table rose into the air and moved toward the head of one of the villains. Both of them gasped and scurried backward, and then they turned and bumped into each other as they tried to get out of the restaurant's door.

"That's three, sir. And I assure you, it is not easy lifting anything, particularly something so heavy, sir."

"So it was you?"

"Did you imagine otherwise, sir?"

"No, I suppose not. And what did you mean by 'That's three'?"

"I've saved your life three times now."

"And what should I do now?"

"Catch the night coach, sir, rather than sleeping here and risking their wrath tomorrow morning."

And as the coach rumbled westward, its jostling making sleep impossible, Swain inhaled to begin to speak and immediately heard, "Yes, sir, I am here."

"You can read my mind, my thoughts."

"Yes, sir, that seems to be the situation. And you may be aware—you are not exactly hearing me with your ears. My words are directly in your mind."

"My imagination?"

"No, sir. Then you'd be mad. No, sir, in your mind."

"But you can appear, like to the . . . lady and, in a way, to the thugs."

"And I can even muster sounds—a few words, sir—if necessary. But all of this is difficult, sir. And I confess, I have no idea how I do it, when I know it must be done. Could you please turn around, sir?"

"You mean in my seat?"

"No, sir. I mean, could you return to Alabama, to pay my wife and perhaps even find my remains? I know that you are carrying a great deal of money sewn into the lining of your portmanteau, sir."

"I sold my property, including my workers, so I could leave the South until the war is over."

"But you are going to have bad luck—and I assure you, that it is not my doing, sir! Bad luck because you have abandoned your home, your people, your responsibilities. I make no judgment myself, sir. But I am aware of this fact, this situation, sir."

"How are you aware? How did you know of the dangers from which you protected me?"

"What I know is that I was on a field that would have been a pleasant place, except for the young men running at each other with fixed bayonets. Sir, it was terrible! I was frightened, more frightened than ever I have been—and frightened of being frightened, of running or hiding, of being punished—and frightened of being hurt so far from home, from my wife, sir.

"And then I felt as though I'd been kicked by a mule. Have you ever been kicked by a mule, sir?"

"By a horse, once."

"Horse, mule—close enough. Then you know, sir, how it hurts, how it prevents one from being able to move."

"Yes. It took me several days—"

"Yes, sir. Well, it didn't give me that opportunity. Because as I lay dying, I looked down at my chest, and blood was pouring from it. And I—oh, it sounds foolish now—I put a finger into the hole, the bullet hole, to try to stop the blood the way one might put a finger into a hole in a broken cup, sir.

"But the blood did not stop. And my vision began to fade, and the brightness of the day darkened, and the noise of the gunshots and the screams of rage and pain and self-deception faded in my ears, sir. And I crawled toward a tree, thinking that somehow I would be safe there.

"And suddenly, everything stopped. Everything was dark, black, sir. But as suddenly, everything was bright beyond belief, as bright as the brightest flash of lightning, sir, but it didn't fade as does lightning, sir. It was and remains—my vision, my world—as bright as lightning. And this confused me even more, sir—at the same time, I could see several distinct images, rather like when there are several people speaking at the same time and you can hear bits of all of the words, sir. But here, I could see, somehow at the same moment, my body as I seemed to float up from it and the Yankee boy who'd shot me, and I saw that he was just loading his weapon and pointing it in the general direction of my fellows, not aiming, not trying to hit anyone, leaving the bullet's destination to fate.

"And I saw, sir, my wife, my widow, suddenly sit up in our—her—bed and scream my name.

"And I saw you, sir, handing the five gold pieces to that agent man on the porch.

"And I not merely have seen such things. I understand them. I understand life, its meaning, more than I could have imagined an ignorant farm boy understanding everything. And I can speak more clearly, with the right words that seem to come to me easily.

"Please, sir, help my wife—my widow. Please return and find her and help her. Give her her money, sir, please."

And so Swain caught a stagecoach heading east. He and the driver and the guard and other passengers rode silently for two days and nights, stopping only to eat and relieve themselves. And then Swain heard, "Sir, you need not worry about my body, my earthly remains."

"No, I'll do what I can if you but tell me where—"

"No, sir. It's not necessary. Although animals ate part of my body, good people went to the battlefield and buried the remains, albeit not knowing our names, and a clergyman prayed over the grave, the huge hole containing young men from both sides."

And Swain shivered as he heard, from a distance, the Rebel Yell but in a minor key, the faint moaning of lost souls gone from their homes, gone from their people, gone from life.

And he heard weeping and knew enough not to say any more.

Days later, they approached a village. "Here, sir. Please get off here."

He did. And he stood in the small settlement, holding his suitcase.

An elderly man approached him, followed by an equally elderly woman. They looked at him. He waited for either to speak; then he said, "I'm looking for—" And as he realized he did not know her name, he heard, "Elizabeth," and he said it aloud.

"How do you know her?" asked the unsmiling man.

"I'm a friend of her husband."

"Which one? Which husband?"

Swain heard a groan, and evidently, so did the old couple.

"Her first."

"What was his name?"

Again, Swain paused momentarily, then, responding to the ghost's voice in his mind, said, "Jesse."

Then, hearing another whisper, he continued, "Drummond. Jesse Drummond."

They led him to the farm of the parents of her second husband, Jacob George. "Don't think about shakin' hands with him," the old man rasped on the way. "He lost his right arm fightin' the Yanks."

And Elizabeth and Jacob looked at him with suspicion. But he slowly held out his clenched fist, which contained three U.S. twenty-dollar gold coins. He handed them to Elizabeth.

"He saved my life. He meant to send you, Mrs. George, a hundred dollars, what he was paid, but you got only fifty. Here's sixty. The extra ten is my gift to you."

"They're Yankee," Jacob muttered.

"However the war turns out, they'll be good someday. Either the Union wins, and they're legal tender again, or we win, and we'll trade with 'em like we do with England and Mexico now."

Jacob looked sternly at Swain and held his hand out beneath Elizabeth's. She dropped the coins onto his open palm. "I'm gonna hide 'em," he said and walked away. "You all stay right here."

When he was out of sight and the old couple was seated on a porch, smoking pipes, Swain took a knotted handkerchief out of his coat pocket and handed it to Elizabeth. "Your husband, Jesse, saved my life at least three times. There's two hundred more dollars in this handkerchief. I don't mean to sound rude, but perhaps you should hide this until you need it."

Eyes wide in amazement, she quickly tucked it in a pocket of her dress.

"I'll go now," said Swain. "Hide it."

She nodded, and Swain turned and walked away.

"Thank you, sir," Swain heard. It was not just Elizabeth's voice, but also that of his ghostly companion.

As Swain walked back toward the road, hoping to find another stage to take him east or west, he heard, "I'll stay here with her, sir. With them. Of course, I'll sleep in the barn . . . stay in the barn, except to help 'em. I don't want to see—"

"I understand. An excellent idea. You'll be like a guardian angel."

"Yes, sir. And I want to say, if I could be in two places at once, I'd want to protect you too, sir. 'Cause I imagine that you'll keep on needing help. Failing my presence, sir, please go cautiously, wherever you go. I'll always be grateful, sir."

"Perhaps we'll meet again somewhere, on this side or where you are."

"Perhaps, sir."

And Swain suddenly heard the faintest swishing sound and felt an emptiness—an emptiness that stayed with him for the rest of his life.

The South, Rise Again

DL Thurston

Another day and Hamilton Dunham was still in Pittsburg Landing. He woke to the late fall sun filtering through the barren branches overhead. Elihu was already gone, driven by the energy of the young. Dunham needed more time to get moving. His bones and joints reminded him of how old he was. Elihu's energy twisted that knife further. Digging through ruined battlefields was a young man's game; it needed someone like Elihu. Shame he wasn't the right man for the work.

He'd woken the last few mornings nearly as exhausted as when he'd gone to sleep the night before. He trusted a breakfast of sooty coffee and hardtack to sustain him until lunch and set out into the Shiloh battlefield. Three days among the dead of Shiloh and he didn't reckon he was more than a third finished. The mornings were getting colder, crisper. It might almost be pleasant if he were here for any other reason than breathing life to the long dead. Greycoat dead. Edmund Whitman made sure of that earlier that summer, taking the *honored* Union dead off to the new federal cemetery. Whitman had federal support, federal money, federal help. He didn't have anyone like Hamilton Dunham. He didn't have a resurrectionist.

Dunham made mental notes of each body he passed as he picked through the trees. That rock was actually a skull. That exposed root was actually a rib. He found Elihu crouched next to Tillman Creek, with a map spread out on a rock. The younger man added his own notations, tracking the retreat of Maj. Gen. Braxton Bragg and his men.

"We went further east," Elihu said. "There was a redoubt here. It ain't anymore. Couldn't go through it. We went around. There's men dead out there." He tapped a spot on the map then pointed through the woods, well outside where Dunham was planning to look.

"You sure?"

"Lost a good buddy nearly at Owl Creek there."

"Then we'll start there today."

The maps were all based on secondhand stories and questionable after-action reports. It was invaluable to have an assistant who was in the battle. Elihu pulled his old grey uniform jacket tight against the chilly wind and took the lead toward Owl Creek. His memory was dead on. By the banks was a skirmish site that the maps forgot and Whitman missed. Blue coats mixed with grey, muddied, and one from the other barely distinguishable. Dunham found a body with captain's bars and carefully turned it over. There was little left of the captain, bones roughly held together by fetid bits of muscle, cloth and mummified skin rotted into one.

"Ready?" Dunham asked.

Elihu swallowed some bile. "No. But go."

Dunham took a deep breath and put his hands on either side of the captain's head. He closed his eyes and concentrated, pushing a little bit of himself into the felled officer. The battle was so long ago; some men were too far gone. The rest were so long dead that waking them wasn't enough. Dunham needed to undo what time had done. Muscle and skin twisted back into place, loosely covering bone. The captain twitched and twisted before taking in a sharp rasping breath and then coughing out stale air that stank of mold. The captain's left eye was long lost to time, and the right rolled blindly in its socket. Dunham couldn't undo nearly so much rot as that, not with how painful tired he was.

"Can you hear me, captain?"

"Who's there?" His voice pushed past a rotted tongue and out a grim lipless smile, but his accent still held the French notes of a bayou accent.

"My name is Hamilton Dunham. We don't have much time. What was your name?"

"How are my men?"

"I'd like to find out, but I need to know your name."

"Chauncey Booream, Seventeenth Louisiana."

Dunham looked up at Elihu, who diligently wrote down every word in a yellowed journal. He returned his attention to Captain Booream. "Do you have any messages for your family?"

"My . . . my family? Am I not going to make it?"

"I'm afraid you already didn't, Captain."

"What? I don't understand." Captain Booream tried to lift his arm but left most of it on the forest floor, buried in rotting leaves.

"Is there any message you want sent?"

"Find my boy, find Benji. Tell him his daddy's proud of him. Tell him to take care of his momma. Tell him we're going to win this war."

Captain Booream coughed again. His chest collapsed with the force, and he screamed in pain. Dunham placed a hand on the man's forehead. "Rest now, Captain. You'll be home in Louisiana soon."

Booream went limp, and he slipped away again into death. Skin retreated, muscle melted away. Dunham let him settle back into the ground. Elihu's pen still scratched over the paper. Dunham stood, his knees popping and groaning. The younger man was charting the area, marking the body of Captain Booream for a later team to recover and repatriate his remains. Dunham surveyed the field, looking over the work ahead of them, and prepared for a long day. He moved to the next man and the next, collecting names, gathering statements, each dutifully transcribed by his young assistant. Some bodies they could identify from personal effects; too many required Dunham's special touch. Each fallen soldier had his position plotted and marked, a map of the death of Shiloh emerging on the pages the two men carried with them. Dunham even checked the bluecoats they found. Whitman may not have shown the fallen Confederates such care, but that didn't mean Dunham had to sink to the same discourtesy.

As they stopped for lunch, Dunham felt the fatigue of the day seeping into his bones. These days got longer, harder. His methods left his mind and body so absolutely spent.

But it was good work. That's what kept him going.

"Mr. Dunham?"

He put his spoon down, welcoming a reason to stop eating. His meal of beans, cooked twice too often, and a scrap of cured jerky, a little more appetizing than shoe leather, could wait. "Yeah?"

"How come you never ask them where they've been?"

"They've been right here. Dead don't go nowhere unless someone moves them."

"That ain't what I meant."

Dunham took another bite of the mushy beans. "I guess it wasn't."

"Then why? They've been to the other side. They know what's out there. They've been to the pearly gates, gotten their reward."

"Have they?"

"You don't believe?"

"Let's say I'd rather not know."

"Aren't you curious?"

Dunham put his spoon down again. "Ever been reading a book? Want to know real bad how it ends?"

"Yeah."

"Ever turn to the end and find out?"

Elihu considered the question. "This is different."

Dunham shook his head. "Ain't no difference. I'd prefer not know how this book ends. Not till it's my time to find out for sure."

Elihu let him finish his meager lunch in peace and kept quiet as they worked their way through the dead of the Seventeenth Louisiana, the Twenty-Third Alabama, and even an officer of the First Arkansas. Dunham considered reprising the conversation but welcomed the silence. It was less worry as he was forced deeper and deeper into his own mind, resurrecting the dead one by one. Some couldn't say but a few words. Others Dunham quieted. Shadows lengthened, and what little warmth the day imparted slipped into an early evening. Dunham's breath now came in clouds. He wanted to wrap up the day and come back to Owl Creek tomorrow. It was then that Elihu broke his silence.

"Butler!"

Elihu scrambled into the deep shadows, leaving the bone-tired Dunham to follow. He found the young Confederate hunched down, cradling a decomposed body, its head resting in his lap. He looked up as Dunham neared. "This is Butler Markell. We mustered up together. I remember when he fell. Knew I'd have to tell his momma."

Dunham rubbed his sore neck. "I'll give you some space."

"Wait."

Dunham turned back.

"Aren't you going to . . . you know."

"That's for the bodies we can't identify."

"Please. Just a few minutes."

Elihu had been so much help scouring the battlefield. Even as Dunham's body said it wasn't in him, he knew he owed something to the young greycoat. Dunham knelt down and focused on waking the dead Markell. The resurrectionist's heart fluttered, and his brain screamed. The body jerked and coughed as Butler Markell came back after so many years dead. He looked around with missing eyes. The recovered skin on his face was stretched tautly; muscles and tendons hung loose about his body, but still, Elihu looked at him with the love engendered by brotherhood in arms. Dunham straightened, his pains grown worse, how they tore at his very essence. He patted Elihu on the shoulder and gave the younger man some privacy. Bits of the conversation floated through the bare trees as he limped toward the campsite, each tree a crutch. The farther he went, the thinner he felt, until he reached his limit and readied a forced campsite.

Dunham lit a fresh fire and set in for a dinner that was equal parts unsatisfying and filling. Somewhere in the dark, he felt Markell slip away again, releasing what bits of Dunham he held on to. Dunham rolled a cigarette, smoked it down, and was halfway through a second before Elihu came through the trees and settled in beside the fire. The sun was long gone; the night was now cold and dark with the twinkle of stars overhead. Elihu sat quietly and stared into the fire, saying nothing.

"You asked, didn't you?"

Elihu wouldn't make eye contact.

"He didn't have an answer, did he?"

"You listened?"

Dunham took another drag from his cigarette then flicked the butt into the fire. He rolled another. "Want one?"

Elihu held out a shaking hand. He clenched the cigarette hard between his teeth, not smoking it, just letting it burn.

"You've asked, haven't you?"

"No." Dunham rubbed the bridge of his nose. "But I know folks who have. Most people do. They always say the same thing."

"Why didn't you tell me?"

"I've told people before. They never believe me, always have to ask for themselves." Dunham lit his new cigarette. "I guess I thought I'd try something different. See if I could get you to not be so damned curious."

Elihu's cigarette smoldered between his fingers. "Does that mean there's nothing?"

Dunham considered his cigarette and replied, "Means no one knows when they come back. I think we ain't meant to know, not till we get there."

"Goddamn."

"Pretty much."

Elihu held his cigarette in his left hand and stared at it hard. The cigarette dropped to the ground; Elihu moved his fingers, watched them. Dunham could feel the exhaustion coursing through his body. He was so close to sleep now.

"Mr. Dunham?" Elihu's voice was distant now.

"Yeah?"

"How'd we do?"

"South surrendered about eighteen months ago."

"Damn."

"Sorry. You've been a real help."

"Are you sending me back now?"

Dunham wiped some sweat from his brow. "I've kept you as long as I can."

Elihu finally looked at Dunham. "I don't remember anything."

"They never do."

He was losing his focus. It had been a long few days. Tomorrow, he'd work alone, and then he'd find another assistant.

"Mr. Dunham?"

"Yeah?"

"You'll make sure I get home?"

"That's why I'm here."

"Thanks."

Dunham felt Elihu slipping away. He couldn't stop it now. Elihu lay down.

"Mr. Dunham?"

"No more questions now."

Dunham took a deep breath and let go. Elihu's body crumpled as he let out one last breath. It was a weight off Dunham's soul but not a relief. He laid out his bedroll alongside the fire and settled in for a sleepless night.

The Dragon and the Shark
David Boop

1868

I t didn't take a genius to know Sebastian Maher would lose the hand if he called the fifty-dollar bet. The person sitting across the felt from him was too confident, and while Maher's cards were good, they weren't that good. Problem was he'd let himself be goaded into betting his entire stack on the two cards he had swapped out. They'd been the cards he wanted, but whatever his nemesis had drawn must have been better. The cowpoke glowed like a streetlight in New Orleans.

This left Maher with two choices: bow out gracefully and try to start over from the last fifty-dollar bill secured in his boot . . . or cheat. Seeing as their riverboat would dock at Memphis in just under an hour, cheating seemed the best course of action.

Maher apologized. "I'm sorry, but I do believe you have me at a disadvantage, sir. I can tell from the way you just cannot contain your enthusiasm that you must have received something special from that last exchange of cards."

"Believe what you want, dandy," his slack-jawed opponent said. "Yer gonna have to pay to see if yer right."

The term *dandy* had been thrown at him before, as if it meant he preferred the company of men or something to that effect. Maher considered himself a gentleman—educated at better schools, bred from better stock. If the cretins south of Saint Louis couldn't tell the difference between a true man of the world and a poof, that was their ignorance.

"Sir, since you're going to take me for all my winnings, then please indulge me a chance to tell you a tale before I have to leave the table. It won't take long, and you might find it fascinating."

The cowpoke, a man who hadn't seen a lick of soap in months, grimaced. "What does *indulge* mean?"

"It means grant me a favor, a boon, if you will." Maher waved his hand in a simple gesture of penitence.

"What does *a boo*—"

"I want to tell you a story."

Maher wondered what ancient god he must have offended to draw only a full house against such a buffoon.

"You tell yer story, then I git all yer money?"

The gambler nodded.

"Fine. Tell yer story. But if I smell any sort of trick, I'll shoot ya where ya stand." The cowpoke placed his gun on top of his cards to emphasize the point.

They were both sitting, but not wanting to play semantics, Maher let the lapse in grammar pass.

Leaning back in his chair, the gambler made sure all eyes were on him as he spoke. He'd done a bit of theatrical training and knew how to capture a crowd.

"A long time ago—a couple hundred years, truth be told— seven men sought the Mississippi River in hopes that it'd lead them to the Pacific Ocean."

A man who'd folded early in the game interrupted, "I know this one. That was them Lewis and Clark fellas."

"Not quite," corrected the gambler. "This was before them. It was led by a French missionary, Jacques Marquette, and a fur trader named Jolliet."

The assembled men and waitresses spat on the floor at the word *French*. They waited to see what Maher would do, a test of his allegiances.

"Oh yes. I forgot." He made a spitting attempt at the floor. "Fuck the French."

That satisfied everyone around him, so he continued. "After they passed the Straits of Mackinac, they encountered a savage tribe of natives. The Illini were fierce warriors, but having encountered other servants of God before, they did not attack the father and his group. Instead, they passed on a warning."

"What type of warning?" asked another player, the one who'd folded last, leaving just Maher and his cowboy opponent. The man swallowed hard, waiting for the answer.

Maher obliged. "They warned the men of a winged beast that would devour whole anyone who dared travel near its nest."

"Git out," said the cowpoke. "Ain't no bird that big in the territories. We'd heard of that by now."

Maher shook a finger at him. "No, sir. This was no bird, but an ancient beast still alive from the dawn of man. A monster left over from the flood that had managed to escape doom and flew above the waves, through the rain, and survived to find land after the waters subsided. It was a creature whose only kin might be the great Leviathan that gobbled Jonah up whole."

Eyes widened, and a few men crossed themselves.

"The good father and the trapper ignored the warning and continued on. It wasn't even three days southbound on the Mississippi until they saw them."

"T-them?" asked the early folder.

"Yes, two of them." Maher used hushed tones as he spoke. "A male and female. They were high on a bluff, overlooking the mighty Miss. They were horrible winged demons with feathers of yellow and green and red and black."

Seeing as he had his audience enthralled, the gambler recited the legend as it'd been told him. "They were as large as young cattle with horns on their heads like those of a deer. Red eyes glared down at them. Each had a beard like a tiger's, one a horrible mannish face, the other a hideous lady's. A long tail that wound all around the bodies, passed above their heads and going back between their legs, ending in fish's tails."

He could see by the shifting of eyes that everyone tried to envision what Father Marquette witnessed.

"The female creature spotted the craft in the water and swooped down to snatch one of the oarsmen from the canoe. Screaming, he was carried back to the nest, where the mates ripped him apart to serve as breakfast for the winged monster's brood, who, incidentally, were just starting to hatch from their eggs."

Maher took off his hat and pressed it against his chest. He bowed his head in reverence, and all did the same. In that moment, Maher quickly switched one of his pair cards with a sleeve card, giving himself four of a kind.

"Deciding they would grab some lunch too, the male started his descent toward the expedition. The remaining men were ready, as was the father who held the Holy Book aloft and prayed for divine intervention. A rain of bullets filled the air between them and the beast. Most bounced off its thick hide, but one, guided by God himself, hit the creature in the eye, where it entered the brain, killing it. It dropped in the big river, and the splash nearly capsized their canoe. Enraged, the female monstrosity dove at the crew, vengeance in her angry red eyes. Trapper Jolliet, seeing a shadow in the water, paddled their canoe quickly over it. When he said the word, all jumped out of the boat as the winged demon crashed into it. Below, a large rock sat waiting. The creature broke its neck and floated to the surface."

Everyone drew a breath of relief. Maher waited for the question someone would eventually ask.

"What happened to those babies?"

"The expedition climbed up the bluff and slew each and every one of them. The end."

There was a round of clapping.

"In honor of your allowing me that reprieve, I will pay to see your cards." Maher reached down and pulled out his last fifty to match the bet. "Call. Let's see how badly I am undone."

The cowpoke returned his mind to the game, having been completely drawn in by the tale. "Um, yeah. Well, I've got a straight flush." He flipped over a seven to jack straight, all of the club variety.

"Oh dear. That is an almost unbeatable hand."

The cowpoke grinned and reached for the pot.

"However, I was sure you had a royal flush when I spoke. I do, indeed, have you beat. Good thing I didn't fold."

Maher flipped over his four queens. The crowd whooped at his success, all save for the cowpoke, who looked angrily at the gambler.

"Yer a goddam cheat, that's what ya are! Ya done distracted us and did some sort of switch." He lifted his gun to aim it at Maher.

"Now, now, kind sir. There were witnesses here. I count a dozen men who stared at me the whole time. When could I have pulled some sort of ruse? At what point did anyone not gaze with rapt attention at me?" He scanned the crowd. "Who saw me touch my cards? Anyone?"

No one answered. No one spoke up. That seemed to anger the cowpoke even more.

"I had ya beat. Ya knows it, and I knows it."

"Well then," said Maher, holding up his hands, "we seem to be at a bit of an impasse. What would you suggest to settle this like men?"

"I suggest I kill you and take my winnings."

"I have a better idea. How about we go up on deck and stage one of those gunfights your breed love so much?"

This brought a round of laughter from the crowd. None would have bet on the gambler to be able to even hold a gun.

The cowpoke laughed too. "Okay. Let's do it yer way. Ya own a gun?"

"Oh, I'm fine. You bring yours, and I'll bring my own weapon." The gambler reached into his sleeve and pulled out a whistle.

This brought more laughter. The cowpoke looked at the small silver object.

"Yer gonna beat me with that?"

Maher nodded. "Shall we be off?" To the dealer, he said, "Please collect the pot and store it until one of us returns."

The deck of the steamboat had enough space for five paces. Both men agreed that would be enough. They stood back-to-back and started counting off. Maher placed the whistle in his mouth and blew it once for each step. On the fifth step, he blew it long and hard.

The cowpoke spun and drew. His finger slid into place, but he never got the chance to pull the trigger before he was lifted off the deck by a creature from nightmares. It had feathers the color of yellow and green and red and black. Its face, a hideous distortion of a woman's, bit down on the cowpoke as she dragged him skyward. His scream was cut short as his body was swallowed whole. The creature disappeared into the night sky before anyone blinked.

"Oh," said Maher as he took in the crowd, "I left off one part of the story. You see, there were two Piasa eggs that hadn't hatched yet." He leaned conspiratorially toward one of the passengers. "Piasa being the Illini Indians' name for the creatures."

Maher straightened back up and continued. "Trapper Jolliet took them and kept them warm, wrapped in pelts. When they hatched, he raised them and trained them. He headed south and hid among the people of Mexico. There, he kept the Piasas, now known as Quetzalcoatls, safe, and with each generation, the oldest male of his line is given a chick to raise as his own personal guardian. Interesting story, right?"

The riverboat passengers nodded.

"Well, looks as if we're getting close to dock. If you all don't mind, I'm going to collect my winnings and catch the next ferry to Little Rock. I hope to make the Arizona Territory in a week. I'm sure I can trust everyone to keep mum about this, right?" He tapped the whistle still sticking out of the corner of his mouth. Again, everyone nodded.

"Thank you all very much for your support. There's a copper mine opened near Drowned Horse, and I expect there will be a card game set up at the local watering hole. Feel free to join me anytime." But he doubted any of the passengers would. If anything, none of them would ever come close to the territory, and that was just dandy with him.

Matty and the Grey Man

Lara Ek

There was five of us till Pappa caught the pneumonia, an then after, there was only four of us, an Mamma had a hard time of it. Starting us turning sixteen she was fixing for us to get married, since no seamstress couldn't hold up three girls an herself on a widow woman's leavings, but there never came nothing of it till Josie, the oldest of us, turned eighteen. That day noon, a big black motorcar come rolling up the road and stopped right in front of our house.

Well, Mamma went out the door to see, an me an my sisters went to the window. Out that car got a tall man in a right smart suit, bald an with a pale, pale face an round dark glasses up against his eyes. Tie grey, suit grey, shirt white, shoes with grey wingtips, pale wood cane wrapped in a white leather handle. He held that tight in his hands as he spoke to our mamma.

Then Mamma turned right round an hustled back inside, busting through the door an crying, "Girls, put on your best an wait in the parlor! Here's Mr. Smith looking to marry a one of you!" An out that window, the grey man looked at us.

Well, we puts on our best and goes down to the parlor an lines up on that couch, whispering who Mr. Smith might be an how an why. An when he come to the door, we all went silent.

"Ms. Josie," said Mr. Smith. "I want you."

"To talk to you on marriage," Mamma says, coming in behind him, an Mr. Smith don't nod nor shake his head—just watched Josie through them round glasses. "Hurry out now," Mamma says to us two young ones, an we gets up an walks out, an the door shuts quiet behind us.

Well, Josie was a pretty girl, sweet as a kitten an quiet as an old mule, an Mr. Smith was a mining man—got plenty of money but no young wife to share it with—an so you already know how that turned out. Mamma said yes, an Josie said yes, an Mr. Smith said nothing but "I'll send money for the wedding dress" an walked out. That wedding was held a week after, an Mr. Smith arrived just fore noon; an he stood in the ceremony, set at the table after, then stood an told Josie, "Wait for me at the gate in a week."

An in a week, Josie met Mr. Smith at the gate, an Mr. Smith drove up in that big black motorcar an took Josie away.

Josie sent one letter. Then we heard nothing no more.

Well, a year later, it was Sadie's birthday when she turned eighteen. An noon that day, there's a big black motorcar comes rolling up the road an stop right in front of our house, an it's Mr. Smith—grey suit, grey tie, pale wood cane with a white leather grip. Mr. Smith got out of that car an come to the door an met Mamma an talked to her, an finally, Mamma come back in an told us, "You girls best put on your clothes an' wait in the parlor. Mr. Smith says Josie got lost in the woods, an he's looking to marry again."

So we puts on our best an waits in the parlour; an pretty soon, the door opens, an there's Mr. Smith. He looks us over slow.

"Ms. Sadie," he says to my sister. "I want you."

"Wants to talk to you on marriage," Mamma says, coming in behind him, an Sadie gets up an curtseys, an Mamma hushes me out of the room.

An Sadie married him, sure enough, though Mamma didn't like it none. But he had the money, an he was awful sorry about Josie, so she shut her mouth an let Sadie off. They had their wedding, though the neighbors was jawing on about it something fierce, about where was Josie an why hadn't there been no funeral. Mr. Smith didn't take no mind—just told Sadie, "Wait for me at the gate a week from now." An Sadie dressed up in that wedding dress and did.

An that day, noon, Mr. Smith come up in his big black motorcar an took Sadie off.

She sent one letter, an then we never heard from her no more.

But I was seventeen by this time, an by the time one year rolls around, I turn eighteen. An that day I did, Mr. Smith showed up again—wearing them same clothes, holding that same cane—an I knowed he come for me. But I set quiet on the parlor couch an waited while Mamma talked to him, an I waited for that moment Mr. Smith showed up at the door an said, "Ms. Matty, I want you."

I stood up, an I said, "Yes, Mr. Smith."

The wedding was a week after, an when the day of it come, Mamma says, "You don't have to, Matty. You can turn right round an leave this man." I tell Mamma I need to find out where's Josie an Sadie, an she says, "Well then, just remember, he got some kinda charms, knowing your birthdays an coming for all three of you. You just watch he don't use 'em on you."

"Oh, he got no charms, Mamma," I says. "He's just uncommon clever. I'll find you Josie an Sadie, an I'll bring them right back no matter what he done."

An so I married Mr. Smith, though it weren't much of a wedding, being hardly any neighbors there an none for his side. He come to the ceremony just in time an barely stayed after—just took a bite off my plate, a drink off my cup—an says to me, "I'll see you in a week at the gate, Ms. Matty."

I said, "Yes, Mr. Smith."

An that week, I was there. That black motorcar came up the road, left black smoke in the yard, an we was off.

We went long in that car—long, long hours, twisting through mountain after mountain—going north and west an I didn't know where. The driver was driving, an Mr. Smith was sitting stretched up, straight up, next to me but not touching, cane under his hands an eyes staring straight ahead. I looked out the window, but there was nothing there to see—just black pine trees, mile after mile; black woods; an sometimes a white thing running in the trees far away.

Finally, we got to his house, cindery brick under black pines, big an windowed, four floors tall an its roof steep an peaked under the thin pine branches. The motorcar drove on up to that front door, an I followed Mr. Smith out the car an in the house.

It was like a house no one lived in. It was clean an nice; it was beautiful. There was art on the walls, there was paintings around, there was sculpted beautiful creatures in the corners, an above us, there was electric lights. They buzzed an hummed as we walked under them, an sometimes they went out, leaving the halls part-dark, turning the paintings grey and black against pale grey walls.

But Mr. Smith never noticed this. He said, "Follow me" an then walked off, deep in the halls of that grey house. An I noticed after a while of walking that they was all alike, all alive with paintings that looked out at you an them white stone creatures an them lights that turned on an off above you. An finally, we got to some rooms with a canopy bed, an Mr. Smith looks around, looks at me, an grins with all his teeth. They was grey an wide-set, a space between each tooth an long like fence posts.

"Here, we got our marriage," he says, an I come forward.

"Yes, Mr. Smith," I says.

"But," he says an stops me by holding my shoulders, "I got some business first. I'd do this, I would, but first, I got business. So you wait three days."

I looks up at him.

"Three days," he says. "An' you can have this house. It's yours. These keys here—here. They's yours. Any room, any hall, any pretty garden of this house an' it's all yours, 'cept for one place. You see this key?" He held it up. One big round ring of keys, all the same shape an size an metal, excepting a small gold key with the hook at the end. "This one, you never *touch*. You never touch, else you never see another day. You hear?"

"Yes, Mr. Smith," I tells him.

He looks at me long, looks me up an down, then grins, gives me the keys, then walks past me back down grey halls to the car that's awaiting where he left it.

An there I am alone, the new bride in the grey hallways with the off-an-on lights an the queer stone creatures an the doors to my room before me.

I went on in; I slept. An in the morning, it's early, but I walks out. That house was considerable big, but I had a mind to find Josie an Sadie, an I walked a long time in those hallways, unlocking door after door. There's some doors just led to empty rooms, nothing but floor an walls an ceiling an not even cobwebs. There's doors led to rooms full of dark wood furniture, most spotless. There's doors led to rooms full of beautiful things, rare stones, raw gold, an piles an heaps of sun-shining jewels. But I had a mind to find Josie an Sadie, an I kep looking.

Looked an looked, an after two days, I found his rooms. The only other ones with beds an the only rooms that look lived-in—they had dust on the floor with all footprints scuffed in it an old stains on the floor an linens no one never bothered wash. I looked through them rooms but nothing extraordinary.

White shirts in the chest, grey suits in the wardrobe, an in a rack on the wall holding all those pale wood canes with white leather wrapping. I look round an was 'bout to go out when I saw another small door.

Wasn't even no real door. It was his mirror, tall as I an set into the wall. It had hinges.

So I goes there, an there, I sees a keyhole along the meet of wall and glass. An that being an uncommon door, I took an awful hankering to see what was in there. I tole myself, *I shouldn't, but there's time left till he comes back.* I tole myself, *I shouldn't, but where's Josie an' Sadie?*

So I took that gold key with the hook, an I opened the door.

An I pull open that door there, bright mirror with a small dark room behind it. Just inside, there's a switch for the electric light, an I steps inside an cut on the light, an I sees:

Josie an Sadie ain't live no more. Dead, hung up on hooks 'mong a score of other ladies once pretty as me an my sisters, but bled-out now like animals. Their blood dripping out their necks an down their faces or legs an pooled on the floor.

I step back, an I step in blood.

I fall.

Keys fell in the blood.

My hands in the blood, trying to stand myself up an find me the keys.

My hands, my hair, an I slam the mirror shut an take the keys an run.

An the room's shut, but my shoes, bloody on the floor, an my bloody hands on the bloody keys an my bloody hair hanging over my forehead.

I flew to my rooms. I washed an washed, an nothing came out. The blood on my hands stained the linens. I wiped at the footprints, but they led right smack to my room. I wiped off the hooked key, but the whole ring was stained. My hair dripped red onto my clothes.

An Mr. Smith come.

I heard him coming down the hall. I heard him back in my room an that blood still on me, an I knew what he was fixing to do. He hadn't never left the house; he'd just been waiting. I pulled on new gloves over my hands an boots over my shoes an a scarf over my hair. I hides the keys.

An Mr. Smith come to my door. He says, "Well, hello, Matty."

"Hello, Mr. Smith," I tells him. An I tells him, "You're early, Mr. Smith."

"My business was done early," he says, coming in. "An what's you've been doing all this time?"

"Oh, walking the house."

"Any particular rooms?"

"Ah, no," I says.

"Well, go on an tell me," he says.

"There's nothing to tell, Mr. Smith."

"Well then, little Matty, take off your gloves."

"But Mr. Smith, my hands are so cold."

"Well then, little Matty, take off your boots."

"But Mr. Smith, my feet are so cold."

"Well then, little Matty, take off your scarf."

"But Mr. Smith, my head is so cold."

"Well then, little Matty, where's my keys?"

"I lost them," I tells him.

He looks round my room, an he looks at the hiding place, an there ain't no lying no more. I goes to the hiding place, an I takes the keys out, an he sees them stained in blood. I takes the scarf an gloves an boots off, an Mr. Smith looks me up an down an smiles like his face was cracking.

"Ah, little Matty, you been in my room."

"That I have," I tells him, an I backs away to the wall.

"Well, what're you aiming to do now, Matty?" he asks.

"Well, you'll see," I tells him, an I holds the keys in two hands.

An Mr. Smith looks at me an takes a step. An his glasses, he takes off an tosses them to the left, an those eyes, they looking at me close, his mouth grinning wide, an he takes a step. An his cane, he takes an tosses to the right, an he takes a step. An he's near me now, those grey eyes staring an grinning, an he takes another step right up to me.

An I draw back, an I throw the keys at him. That little gold hook goes to gouge him, an he steps back; an I ducks round him an takes up his glasses, crush them in a hand, an throw them in his face, an he steps back. An those grinning, staring eyes finally shut, all glass in them, an I runs to the cane an takes it an turns, an he steps toward me, opens bleeding eyes to me just as I takes the cane an *wham* into his head.

Then he falls an never rises no more.

An I steps forward.

Take the keys up, pull that bloody gold hook out of him. Josie an Sadie, I thinks, an I goes on out.

Railroad Bill

Janice Croom

John hunted the black sheep for three days through the piney woods, across the railroad tracks, and back to his farm. Hunger ached in his stomach like somebody had took a shovel and dug a hole in it. That ache wouldn't let up and musta made him addle-brained. Every time he got close enough to the sheep to take his shot, it seemed like it up and disappeared on him.

Now the black sheep stood in the middle of his cotton field and dared him to shoot it. The weevils were there too, covering every stalk, laying claim to all his hard work, having themselves a fine time eating up his life.

The sheep was downright fat, like it'd feasted on fine grain. Wasn't nothing like the walking bags of bones that lived in these woods fore they all got et.

One clean shot would take the sheep down. One shot to that round speck of white, smack-dab in the middle of its forehead, taunting him like a bull's-eye. One shot and he could feed the chillun something besides mud cakes. With only three bullets left and no way to get more, one shot was all he could spare.

"Don't know where you come from, Mr. Sheep, or how you got so fine and fat, but you 'bout to die."

He crept closer, careful not to step on a root or anything that might make a noise and spook it. The dried pine needles proved a fair cushion. Took a long time to set up his shot. Finally, when he had the sheep dead to rights, he sent a bullet right to that white patch. Dropped that sheep right then and there. Least he should have. When he got to where that sheep shoulda laid stone-cold dead, wasn't nothing there 'cept the weevils.

Didn't take no time to cross the weevil fields to his shack. Couldn't rightly call them cotton fields no more since the weevils had staked their claim. Every year, Sarah had made him set land aside for a garden. With her gone, he'd planted cotton all the way to the door. Couldn't have made a bigger mess if he'd tried.

No cotton meant no money, no credit at Mr. Bob's store, and no food for the chillun. Same thing was happening all through the county. If it wasn't for bad luck, seemed like the colored wouldn't have any luck at all.

His little family waited for him outside on the porch. T-Momma made sure the chillun got a fair amount of sunshine every day. "Don't want them coming down with the rickets," she'd say. So she'd sweep the porch free of weevils, and they'd sit a spell. Used to make John feel all kinds of good seeing his little family out there, but instead of his Sarah fixin' dinner in the kitchen, she lay a-molderin' in the grave. And the rest of the family . . .

Six-year-old Benjamin sat on the edge of the porch, legs almost long enough now to touch the ground. Pants too short. Face too thin. Fore all this trouble, Benjamin woulda run to meet his poppa. He hadn't had strength enough to run for quite a spell.

T-Momma rocked in the chair John had made her, two-year-old Addie in her lap. Addie couldn't stop fretting and fussing. Took her first steps 'bout six months ago. Walked so little now, she might forget how.

Man's s'posed to provide for his family. That's the natural order of things. If he didn't get them some decent food soon, he'd lose them like he'd lost their ma.

The one step twixt the ground and porch creaked when John climbed it. Benjamin's brown face looked from the bag hanging all limp from John's shoulder to the weevils. Chile may have been only six, but he knowed nothing when he saw it.

"Heard a shot," T-Momma said. "Did you get it?"

John laid the gun on the porch. "Wasn't nothing to get. Thought I saw a sheep. Fine and fat as you please. Thought I shot it dead to rights. Musta wanted it so bad I dreamt it."

"Wasn't a black sheep, was it?" T-Momma's crooked finger traced a circle on her forehead. "With a white spot right 'bout here?"

John nodded to keep the peace. Since what he'd seen wasn't real, what difference did a spot in a dream make?

"Go on, carry the baby in the house, Benjamin, and y'all take a nap," T-Momma said. "I'll come get you when it's time to eat."

It hurt John's heart to see Benjamin shuffle to T-Momma like an old man. After they broke the hold Addie had on T-Momma, Benjamin took Addie by the hand and led her into the house.

"No need getting the baby's hopes up case I'm wrong," T-Momma said. "Where did you see this sheep?"

"On the far side of the field."

T-Momma lifted her hands. "Thank you, Jesus. That sheep will save us."

Oh Lord, John didn't know what he'd do if T-Momma had gone addle-brained too. Who would stay with the chillun? "Wasn't no sheep," he said.

"Course there wasn't no sheep. Ain't nobody round these parts ever have no sheep, let alone black ones. Ain't nobody round these parts got food enough to make nothing fat. What you seen wasn't no sheep. What you seen was Railroad Bill."

Fore she married Poppa and moved to Alabama, T-Momma lived in the swamps of Louisiana and brung everything she learned there with her. Ever since he could remember, she hung a mirror right by the door so the devil couldn't get in. Made them eat the middle of a loaf of bread first. Said that way they'd always be able to make ends meet . . .

Mirrors hadn't kept the devil from bringing the weevils, and they hadn't had no parts of no kind of bread for way too long. Railroad Bill was probably just more of her gris-gris foolishness. John didn't want to hear it but wouldn't have nothing like peace until he did.

T-Momma leaned back in her chair and closed her eyes. John sighed and settled on the porch praying this wouldn't take much time. He wanted to get a little sleep fore he went out hunting again.

"First heard about Railroad Bill back when me and your poppa was courting," she said. "Old Bill rode the rails like lots of colored did back then, 'cepting Bill didn't just ride the rails, he robbed the rails. Broke into those crates on the freight train, took whatever he wanted, then threw it out on the track so he could come back and get it later. Sold whatever he got to colored folks for little or nothing.

"Well, sir, the white folks pitched a fit 'bout this colored man robbing them, so they sent a posse to try and track him down. Took 'em three years fore they finally got Bill on account of him being a conjure man. Could turn himself into a fox or a bloodhound or that fat sheep you saw.

"One of Bill's own friends told the sheriff where to find him just like Judas done Jesus, and they shot him dead fore he could change himself into one of his animal forms and get away. The white folks was so proud of themselves they strapped his body to a board and took it to every colored waiting room from Brewton, Alabama, to Pensacola, Florida. Your poppa and me seen it in Montgomery."

"Since you seen the body, you know he's dead. A dead man can't help us."

"'Cepting he ain't dead. I seen him strapped to that board, sure 'nough, but that ain't the end of the story. Not long after that, folks down on they luck started talking 'bout seeing a black sheep with a round white spot on his head. Folks remembered that a sheep was one of the animals Railroad Bill could conjure himself into and started asking the sheep to help them. Folks who asked started getting help. Money to pay they rent. Food to fill they bellies. Railroad Bill showed up when they couldn't get help from nobody else."

"Now he done come to save us. You go find Railroad Bill. Lay your gun down—Bill don't cotton much to guns since they shot all those holes in him—and ask him to help us. Bill will make sure we get everything we need long as you believe . . ."

John nodded off fore T-Momma finished talking about Railroad Bill. He didn't have time to listen to such foolishness. He needed to rest a spell then go back out and try to find something for them all to eat.

For the next two weeks, John went out every day. He didn't find no birds. He didn't find no rabbits. He did spot that black sheep. Shot at it just like before. Even though he knowed he hit it, seemed like that black sheep just would not die.

T-Momma took to her bed. Addie lay beside her. Poor baby didn't even fuss anymore, just stared into nothing.

Benjamin had stopped crying sometime yesterday. Flies circled round him like buzzards. Poor baby too weak to swat them.

John gave up on hunting. Since his babies only had a little bit more time left in this world, he decided to wait for the end with them so they wouldn't die alone. Make sure they had a decent burial, then use his last bullet on himself.

John couldn't shake what T-Momma had told him 'bout Railroad Bill. What if it was true? What if his chillun and momma died on account of him being too proud or too stupid to get them help? He set out to find that black sheep one more time.

John crossed the field, the railroad tracks and went into the piney woods. One minute, he didn't see nothing but pine trees, and in the next, the black sheep stood between those trees, close enough that it wouldn't be no problem for John to pick him off. That's not what he come here to do.

John sat his gun on the ground. He'd never been big on words, so it took a bit to figure out what he wanted to say. "I don't know what kind of powers you got, but I do know I done shot you twice and you ain't dead. If you can help my family, I'd be mighty grateful."

They wasn't the prettiest words, but they was the best he had. The sheep stood there, fixated on him, then disappeared. This time, John knew he wasn't addle-brained. That sheep had naturally disappeared. Since John had done what T-Momma tole him, he thought food would appear just like that sheep had disappeared. He waited and waited, but nothing happened.

John left the piney woods and headed home, praying he'd get there fore his chillun drew their last breath. He just come up on the railroad tracks when he saw it. Scattered on either side of the tracks, where the trains couldn't get to it, were crates of food. Canned soup and vegetables. Sacks of flour and sugar. Some folks might say that they fell off the train, but John knew that somehow Railroad Bill had throwed them off.

"Thank you, Mr. Railroad Bill," he said and then hurried home to feed his family.

Passage

Daniel Powell

The man and his son lived deep in the hill country of the Chattahoochee National Forest. The boy was tall and thin and corded through with muscle; newly sixteen, he stood on the cusp of manhood.

"I just don't understand, Dad," Nathaniel said. "Why do I have to go *tonight*?"

"It's the way it's always been, Nate," the man grunted, averting his eyes from his son's direct gaze. The man's name was Caleb. He had thick forearms and broad shoulders, bushy black hair going to grey, and clear brown eyes. "Always happens on the first full moon in the summer of the sixteenth year. Someday, when you have a son of your own, maybe you'll understand."

"Would you at least tell me a little more about him?"

The man sighed. "His name's Aldous—Aldous McGrane. He's a mountain man—one of the original hilltoppers in this part of the country. He's . . . well, he's been on the mountain a long damned time."

"How long?"

The man shrugged. "Can't say for sure. He used to have a brother, but there was a falling out. Something about a woman."

"And why do I have to meet him?"

Caleb put his elbows on the table, folded his hands, and stared at his son. His expression softened. "Because I want what's best for you, boy. Let me ask you a question: Is this a good life for you? I mean, is it what you want—scratching by and making do up here in the hills?"

The boy pondered the question. His eyes darted around the cabin. It was a simple, comfortable home. One large room up front, two smaller rooms in the back. On the other side of the screened windows, insects fluttered in the gathering twilight.

"I love it, Dad. I don't think I'd ever want to live down in Dalton."

The man nodded. "Well then, consider this your initiation, son. Aldous McGrane just wants a few words with you. I've heard he's near death, but I don't believe it. I reckon he's crisp as a December morning. He knows you work the pine stands with your old man—he'll be interested in chatting with you."

"And it has to be tonight?"

The man nodded. "Tonight."

"An initiation?"

"An initiation, son. Kind of like a test."

"How do I find his place?"

The man smiled; it was an odd expression. The boy caught, in that fraction of a moment, a glimpse of his father that was foreign to him. There was cunning there, and it frightened him.

"Take the Pinhoti Trail clear around the long wall. Head north until you pass through that big ol' marshy slough. You know the one I mean?"

The boy nodded. He'd spent many afternoons catching frogs and snakes there.

"Good. Keep your eyes open, son. It's a slim little trail—cut just so into the brush. You'll find it just ahead of that big blueberry patch. Follow that trail about a mile, and you'll find his place." The man gazed out the kitchen window. The sun still shone—a great ball of shimmering orange on the western horizon—but it was sinking quickly into a pink abyss. "You ought to get a move on."

"What'll I need? I mean, beyond a lantern—"

"No lantern," the man interrupted. "The moon'll be plenty bright." He stood and went to the mantle. With a small silver key he kept on a string around his neck, he unlocked a worn chest and rummaged inside until he found it. "Here—you'll need this."

He went to his son and unclenched his fist. There, in the palm of his calloused hand, was a shiny silver ring.

"McGrane might ask for something—a sort of . . . a gift, I suppose. Don't offer anything until he does. *If* he asks," the man paused, staring into his son's eyes, "then you can give him this." As the words left his lips, he looked away. For the second time that night, the boy saw something in his father that startled him. This time, he saw shame.

"Okay, Dad. I'll give it to him."

The words seemed to sting the man; he darted forward and pulled his son into a close embrace. "You're very bright, Nate. You have your mother's wits, God rest her soul. I know you'll do just fine tonight. I expect to see you back here before morning."

The boy nodded. "I better . . . I guess I better go." He extricated himself from his father's embrace, slipped the ring into his pocket, and stood from the table. "Be back in a little while, Dad."

The man watched his son, his eyes hooded, and merely nodded in reply.

It was an easy walk through beautiful country. Twilight and a little breeze had cooled the air, and the boy made good time on the trail. When he arrived at the wall, he paused to consider it. It was a mystery, that wall—not unlike the errand he was on. Where had it come from? It spanned over nine hundred feet, rising from the Georgia clay like a spine of piled granite.

Some claimed it had been Indians; others said it was an old Viking prince that had built the thing. One legend said it had been built by slaves (some went so far as to call them zombies) working under the conjuration of a Haitian witch.

Nate hurried down its length, wary of touching it (he saw no sense in tempting fate), and picked the trail up on the far side. The path dipped down into a little valley, where the soil squelched beneath his feet. Bullfrogs barked all around him. Doves cooed. Bats flitted about in pursuit of mosquitoes. He hurried through the swamp until the ground became solid, and he stopped in the last of the twilight to pick a handful of blueberries.

He ate some of the berries while the moon rose behind him. It was a silver dinner plate just above the eastern hills, casting pale light over the land.

He picked another handful of berries, stowing it carefully in his pocket, and began searching for the trailhead. After a time, he was on his way again, striding through forest so dense that the brush clutched at his arms and legs as he walked.

The trail crested a slight hill before sliding into a low clearing. There, in the center of a meadow bordered on three sides by pine forest, stood an ancient log cabin. A sagging roof sheltered a dilapidated porch; a thin wisp of smoke escaped the crumbling stone chimney. The lone front window glowed with a sickly yellow light.

The boy descended into the valley and up to the front door, his heart racing. He took a deep breath and extended his fist to knock, but the door sprang open, and a man who looked like he could have built the old wall—he was *that* old—stood before him.

"Nathaniel," he croaked, "come in, m'boy." He reached forward and pulled him inside by the wrist. The old man's strength was shocking. "I knew you'd come. Your father—he's a gambling man, is he not?"

"I don't know," the boy replied. *Was he?* "I don't think so."

Aldous McGrane laughed. "Funny how we don't really *know* the ones we hold closest, eh, boy? Come in, come in."

He closed the door and scurried across the room; he took his seat in a chair by the fireplace. He was stoop-shouldered and frail, and he extended a bony index finger to the empty chair. "So . . . did you bring me a gift?"

The boy nodded eagerly. He went into his pocket, carefully extracting the blueberries in order to reach the ring at the bottom.

"Blueberries?" the old man spat. The contempt in his voice was a living thing, his anger like a cloud of wasps hovering around him. He sprang from his chair and charged across the room. "He told you to . . . to give me *blueberries?*"

"I—"

"That scoundrel!" he said, staring into the fire. "That . . . that thief. Blueberries!" He turned his attention to the boy. "Give them here! I'll have them. If it's blueberries he'll give, then it's blueberries I'll take!"

He snatched at the berries, spilling most of them, and crammed them into his mouth. Nathaniel dug in his pocket for the rest of them, careful not to reveal the ring. He watched as the man took the last of them and shoved them into his mouth. He chewed with ancient yellow teeth, purple juice spilling out over the canvas of wrinkles surrounding thin lips. The man chewed with vigor, staring into the glowing coals popping in the hearth, that purple muzzle expanding on his face. "*Blueberries,*" he muttered, returning to his chair. There was hatred in his eyes. Hatred and sorrow.

The boy sat, wary, and they endured a long and awkward silence. When the old man looked up, his entire demeanor had shifted. "Then he's made his choice, your father has. Good for him! Good for *you*! You know, I've known Caleb now for many, many years."

"Then you must have known my mother."

"Aye," McGrane smile ruefully. "Indeed, I did. A wonderful woman, she was. So sad to pass so early. And to miss seeing her beautiful boy become so strong. So . . . so healthy!"

The boy looked away. Something was wrong with the old man—something beyond mere senility.

"Tell me, Nathaniel—how is it that you've grown to be so strong and healthy?"

"I work in the woods with my father. It keeps me fit."

The old man nodded. "Yes, yes . . . I suppose it does. Do you know . . . do you have any idea how spiders stay fit?"

The boy shook his head, a little smile on his face.

"They *eat* each other—they *consume* one another's bodies." He shuffled into the kitchen. On the sill, there were a dozen or more jars. He took one down and handed it to the boy. There were tiny holes in the lid. "And what is that?"

The boy studied it. A plump black spider with a crimson hourglass on its abdomen reared back at the sudden jostling. "It's a black widow."

"And do you know how it came across that name?"

"They eat their mates."

The old man took the jar and slipped it into the breast pocket of his shirt. He clapped his hands with delight. "Such a bright lad! Caleb must be very proud. Tell me, Nathaniel. Have you had your dinner?"

"I did—I ate with Father before I came to visit you. There's no need to trouble yourself, sir." He was suddenly aware of a lingering odor. Something was cooking in the oven.

"The two of you ate together, eh? That's at least commendable on your father's part. He didn't send you hungry. Good for him. But you must dine with me as well, Nathaniel. I am old and feeble, and I have so few visitors. And you've come all this way to see *me*—the oldest of the Georgia hilltoppers! Eat with me, Nathaniel. I hate to dine by myself."

The boy swallowed thickly. "I'm not hungry . . ."

"Nonsense," the man said, making a dismissive gesture before scurrying over to the stove. "I *insist*."

He found a potholder, opened the hatch on the wood-fired stove, and withdrew a steaming pie. "It's an old family recipe. A kind of a—a Brunswick stew."

While the old man divided the pie and spooned portions onto plates, the boy's mind raced. What did the old man mean about his father being a gambler? Why had the berries made him so angry?

He pulled the ring from his pocket. He was studying it when the old man surprised him.

"What have you got there, boy? What's that?"

Instinctively, the boy slipped the ring into his mouth. "Blueberry. I had one left over."

The man just shook his head in dismay, turning his attention back to his task.

Furtively, the boy withdrew the ring. He reached to the ground and pushed it into a knothole in the soft wooden floorboards.

"Here. We. *Go*," the old man said. He placed the plates on the kitchen table. "Come, come. Let's eat before it gets cold."

They sat, and the old man dug heartily into his meal. Chunks of meat and sliced vegetables mingled in a kind of gravy beneath a pastry crust. It looked pretty good, and the old man was devouring it with great relish.

The boy pushed his portion around with his fork. "My father said that coming to see you . . . well, that it was like an initiation. That all the old hilltoppers did it."

"Said that, did he? Well, I suppose it's true. Won't be long before it's *your* old man they'll be visiting. Everybody passes on, you know. It's natural. But some . . . well, some just pass *through*."

The man turned his head and barked a rapid series of guttural phrases.

Nathaniel felt cold fingers on his neck, a sensation that jolted fear all through him, clear to the marrow in his bones.

"What was that, Mr. McGrane? What did you just . . . were those *words*?"

The old man nodded. "Creek Indian. Muskogee is the actual name for the language. Same folks that built the old wall. Like I said, boy—some of us just pass *through*."

The boy sighed. Unbidden, an image of his mother flashed through his mind.

"Not hungry?" the man said. "I'll take your portion if you don't want it."

The boy shook his head to clear his thoughts. He brought a spoonful of the stew to his mouth. The food was good. "What's in this?"

"Squirrel meat, carrots, and spuds," the man said. "And blood."

"Blood?"

"Yes. *My* blood. Like I said, it's an old family recipe." Like a trap levering closed, he lunged across the table. He took the boy's wrist in his hand and spat another string of words.

The boy saw two things before the world went dark: the clear, infinite pools of the old man's blue eyes and the yellow teeth in his grinning hungry mouth.

THE OLD WEIRD SOUTH

When he regained consciousness, the first thing the boy saw was himself.

Nathaniel (Me? *Is that . . . me?*) was standing before a dusty mirror, wearing his own familiar grin on his own familiar face. He saw himself bend at the knee and jump toward the ceiling; he saw himself touch a support beam, laying the flat of his palm there.

"Outstanding!" He saw himself shout. "Such energy! Oh, this will do just fine, boy!"

Nathaniel looked down. Through blurred vision, he saw that the hands now attached to his wrists were gnarled claws covered in spotted paper-thin skin. His knuckles were knotty arthritic bulbs. He touched his new fingers to his sunken cheeks.

His heart fluttered in his chest. Who *was* he?

"I worried," Aldous McGrane said to him. While the words carried forth from his own mouth, it was clear that they belonged to McGrane. He suddenly knew, with perfect, awful clarity, what had happened. "I worried that you wouldn't break bread with me, boy. See that?"

He pointed to the clock. It showed nine minutes before midnight. How long had he been unconscious? "That's all the time you have left. And I mean *all* of it! You know what? I was resigned to everything that had happened. I was sure that he'd warned you off. But I should have known better! That's not Caleb. My brother—your *father*—is a selfish man. He took the only woman I ever loved, and he stole the greatest gift she'd ever given me."

McGrane continued, "And now I'm going to take what's mine. I'm going down the mountain, and I'll have my ring. Old Caleb—I can't wait to see the look on his face when his dear son returns home from the top o' the hill!"

"He doesn't have it," the boy wheezed. Shooting pains tore through his chest. Breathing was a chore. "My father—he doesn't have the ring."

"What do you mean?" McGrane snarled. The boy was frightened—frightened by himself, by the hateful faces he could make. In his own visage, he saw a mask of anger and frustration. "Where is it?"

"Trade me back."

McGrane laughed. It turned to howling as he was so entertained by the proposition. "Trade you back? Six minutes, Nathaniel. Six . . . fleeting . . . minutes. Fathers and sons. Brothers and nephews. How do you think it is that we've managed to be up here in the hills so long?"

"But a lifetime without your ring is the alternative. My father gave it to me. He told me to give it to you, and if you really want it back, then you need to choose, old man," the boy said. He felt his left arm going numb. A searing heat blossomed in his chest.

McGrane was uncertain. He paced the room for a long minute. "Caleb doesn't know where it is?"

Nate nodded.

"And you do?"

"Yes. If I . . . if I go, you'll never find it. *Never.*"

An expression of grief and sorrow washed over McGrane's face, and he sprinted across the room—stricken. "Do you promise, boy? Do you promise you'll give it to me?"

The boy nodded, and the man scooped the food into his mouth with his fingers; the boy followed suit.

"Do it now," Nate hissed, "or you'll never see the ring again."

With three minutes on the clock, McGrane muttered the words.

There was a momentary blackout—a sense of pervasive nausea and deep despair—and then he was whole again, complete in his own skin. He touched his cheeks, pinched his forearm.

"Hurry!" the old man gasped. He lay prone on the table, hand outstretched. The boy raced to the knothole, retrieved the ring, and placed it in his hand.

"Oh," McGrane said. A reverent quality came into his tone. "Oh my. It's still so beautiful. *She* was so beautiful."

He turned the ring over in his palm as the seconds marched off the clock. At a minute before midnight, the boy asked his question.

"Whose was it?"

"She was my wife," McGrane said. "Many, many years ago, before there was a wall in the forest, *she* gave me this ring. Then my brother . . ." He shook his head sadly. "You know, I see Caleb in your face, Nathaniel. Be wary of him. He's as old as I am, and he was willing to trade you away tonight—to keep his place here on the mountain. We've *both* made our sacrifices— him and me. And even though he gave you the ring, he was willing to risk losing you. Family can be the ultimate betrayal, boy. Don't you ever forget it."

A shudder raced through the old man. His eyes grew cloudy. "I think it's time that I finally met up with her again. You tell Caleb that his brother is gone. You tell him . . . tell him *he's* the old man of the mountain now."

And with the strike of midnight, a final breath slipped between Aldous McGrane's ancient lips. He slumped forward, the ring clutched in his right hand.

The boy stood. He surveyed the old man's cabin for a long moment. He considered returning the ring to his father but then thought better of it.

It wasn't his father's ring anyway. All along, it had belonged to someone else.

He retraced his steps back to the edge of the clearing where his own home stood. From beneath a fan of bright stars, he watched his father's pipe throw orange signal flares into the shadows of the front porch.

He loved his father, and he understood that love deep inside his heart, but now he was frightened of the man. The reality of what his father was—of the sacrifices he'd been willing to make to maintain the balance of his existence on the mountain—suddenly grew clear to him, and he felt sick to his stomach.

How long had they been trading—these two ancient spirits? How long had they been . . . had they been *taking*?

In the dark of the woods, a dove cried out. An instant later, the call was answered in kind. Nathaniel watched his father smoking for another minute then turned and began the long walk into Dalton and the life that awaited him on the far side of the mountain.

Caleb lingered in the inky night for a long time. Something was different. Something had changed. Three times he packed his pipe, his eyes darting occasionally to the pathway.

Nate would return, or he would not. It was all so hard to reconcile.

When the first indigo hues hinted at the coming dawn, he stood and went inside. He paused once, just briefly, in front of the mirror to study his face. The wrinkles around his eyes and mouth were more clearly defined, and the silver in his hair seemed just a shade brighter.

The boy would not return, it seemed, regardless of the outcome.

Caleb went to his bed; he slid beneath the covers. His brother was gone, and now so was his son. In sixteen years, when he was the oldest hilltopper still remaining in the woods of Georgia, there would be no new vessel—no late-night knock at his door promising youth and rejuvenation.

Instead, the ferryman's toll, finally payable after all these years, would mark his final passage.

The Devil at the Crossroads
Wenonah Lyon

The kid's bare feet made puff-puff-puffs of dust in the dirt road. He'd abandoned his shoes a mile or so back. They were too small, and the blister on the back of his heel burst. He stopped for a minute and set down the twelve-string guitar.

He'd looked at stories, songs, and television. Then he used a map and common sense. There were a lot of crossroads, and here was where common sense came in. Any fool should know you couldn't summon the devil in the middle of a highway intersection.

He found a place that looked good, one where he could ride the bus to the end of the line and start walking. Foot miles were further than map miles, but he'd get there before midnight.

It was the dark of the moon, the trees' branches that met over the road cutting out the little light there was. Starlight seemed bright after the tunnel of trees when he came to the crossroads: two country roads forming a cross.

Should he sit in the middle, or was that where the devil popped out? He decided to play it safe and sit a few feet back. He sat cross-legged and tuned his guitar to a C tuning. He ran up and down the strings using his knife as a slide. First, he played "Looky Looky Yonder." Then he slid into "Midnight Special," then "John Henry."

The boy's voice was another instrument. He started singing "John the Revelator," and his fingers drummed on the top of the guitar.

He stopped and wiped his face.

"Boy," he heard a voice say, "you are not at a Baptist church meeting with fat mamas testifying for the Lord. You are at the crossroads to meet me, I assume, and negotiate over your soul. The only less appropriate song is 'Amazing Grace.'"

The boy looked up. A fine-looking man stood in the center of the crossroads, black as the ace of spades, dressed in black linen pants and a white cotton shirt, blousy and full so he could move his shoulders and arms. The boy was disappointed. He sighed.

"What's wrong, boy? Cat got your tongue?"

"I always kind of hoped you was white," the boy said.

"This better?" He looked like Fred Astaire. "I try to make my clients comfortable."

"Are you really a little red devil with a pitchfork and a long tail?"

"I'm a spirit, not a cartoon."

"Would you go back to the black guy then? I'd rather you looked like a pimp than one of those jerks whose eyes don't see me."

The devil shifted back to his first form and said, "You're trying my patience. I suppose you want to challenge me to a guitar match and wager your soul for the ability to play like the devil himself."

"I want to play like myself, not somebody else. Don't mean to be rude, sir, but I want to play what I can—me—work at it, earn my music. Getting it handed to me . . . might as well just buy a record."

"Hmm," the devil said. Now the devil created the Protestant ethic. He's the patron of noncommissioned officers. It's angels that float around on clouds doing nothing all day long. He thought the boy might deserve a bit more investigation.

"What's your name?"

"James Conroy, sir."

Boy was polite too.

"So why are you here, James? Instant fame and fortune?"

"Wouldn't say no, but that's not what I'm looking for."

"What do you want? To sit here and play twenty questions until sunup?"

"It's my guitar, sir. Gone as far as I can on this one."

"It's a poor musician that blames his instrument," the devil said.

"It won't stay in tune because the pegs are old and slip. The strings are deader than dead. It's missing some frets. See this part? The bridge is loose, and I gotta put a matchbook cover under the center, right there, or it buzzes."

The devil took the guitar and sighted down the neck. "The fingerboard's warped as well. Twelve strings put a lot of pressure on a guitar. The top is pulling up. Twelve strings, unless they're very fine instruments, have a short life."

"You got a twelve-string?" James asked.

A twelve-string appeared in the devil's hand. "Twelve-string and fiddle are my instruments of choice."

He handed the boy the guitar. "This guitar is Lead Belly's Stella."

"Did you steal it offen him?" the boy asked.

"I would never take a man's instrument. Some junkie broke in, stole it, and pawned it. One of my minions saw it in a pawnshop for twenty dollars. This twelve-string was made by Pardini himself. Here." He handed the guitar to the boy. "Go ahead, play . . ."

The devil handed him the top of a whiskey bottle. "Here's my slide. Now that was made in hell. It's the top of Jack Daniel's bottles, black Jack, not that green label shit. Broke off in a barroom fight when one lowlife killed another over something too trivial to spit at."

The boy slid the slide up and down the strings, picking—quick, quick, quick—at treble strings and thrumming down the base strings hard, and he could feel the drumming drone reverberate through his chest.

"Jesus H. Christ!" the boy said.

"No profanity. I don't hold with profanity."

"Wasn't profanity! It was a prayer, saying, 'Thank you, Jesus, for making such splendid sounds.'"

"Had nothing to do with Jesus. I admit I like a bit of Mozart, a little Bach now and again. But the blues are my music. I'm a bluesman. Him upstairs? I've caught him listening at the door. Not the Father. The Son. But we're not here for theological discussions. We're here to play, boy."

"Yes, sir."

"We got to get our contract sorted out. What do you want? If you win, you want my Stella?"

"That seems like a reasonable bet," the boy said reluctantly. "But not really . . . first, when you said you ought not to take a musician's instrument, it sounded right. Also, I like this guitar. I owe it. It's taken me a long way. It's got sentimental value as well. But I don't see how I can go much further unless it's fixed. New frets, new tuning pegs, new saddle and bridge. Plus you unwarp the fingerboard."

The devil thought it over. "You know, you could get a job and get all this done for around six hundred dollars."

"Who'd hire me?" the kid said. "I read good enough to fill in an unemployment form. Not much better. Quit school for reasons that are none of your business when I was twelve. I'm short, walk with a limp. I got jug ears. I'm ugly as sin, so they say."

"I wouldn't call you handsome. But I, the Father of Lies, will tell you true—you got a certain charm and nice brown eyes. And you got very big feet and a big nose, and you know what they say about big feet, big nose means big . . . ," the devil trailed off delicately.

The boy blushed. "Thank you. But nobody else notices my pretty brown eyes. Jobs are not, realistically speaking, open to me."

"Steal," the devil suggested. "Better'n losing your soul."

"I promised the man give me this guitar I'd never steal 'less it was food when I was starvin'. I don't go back on my word, especially to a dead man."

The devil was amused. "But this is a kind of starvation. Not of the belly but of the heart. You need to create, need to make music like other men need to eat."

For a moment, the boy was confused. "No. A promise is a promise. You're talking wiggle room, lookin' wormlike for a way of getting out of your given word. No stealin' except for food, that's what I said and that's what I meant."

"James, I don't mean to be hard, but hell is not for you. Trust me, you wouldn't fit in."

The boy looked mulish. "I walked all the way out here oozin' blood from my blister. I got rights. You don't have no choice. You got to have the contest and bet me and beat me. All the songs say so."

"All right then. We'll play." The devil hesitated then said, "Give me your guitar. Best you play with one you know, shit poor as it is. I'll fix it for you."

The devil took the guitar, looked at it long and hard, and handed it back to the boy.

The boy stroked the strings and listened to the true mellow tones. His fingers slid over the frets like butter over hot corn. "True G," he muttered. "True tones." He smiled. "My guitar and I thank you, sir. I didn't mean to be disrespectful. But music's all I got, and if I can't make music, I might as well be in hell."

"You first or me?" the devil asked.

"You," the boy decided. "Ain't never seen no good players live. Maybe I'll pick up something."

The devil started to play. He started with a little tune plucked on the treble strings—a sad little tune in a minor key—something lost, not forgotten, never found. The slide came in, up and down, wailing, the sound of gulls at sea, battered by the winds. Then it was darker, dark as a sky when there was no moon, no stars; and the guitar began to moan, to howl, the despair of the junkyard dog, chained, badly fed, kicked to make him vicious. Dumb beast, dumb pain, living in a dumb universe.

The devil took everything that made up hell and imposed order on chaos.

He finished. "Play, boy."

The boy picked up his guitar. *I can never beat that*, he thought, *and I don't care. This has been the best night of my life.*

He started lyrically, delicately fingerpicking like Mississippi John Hurt—"Candy Man." He wandered through songs and styles, delighting in his newly repaired guitar. He ended with "Make Me a Pallet on Your Floor." Dark had turned to grey, the sun dawning, light creeping up on the crossroads.

Reluctantly, he offered the devil his guitar. "Thank you. In hell, sometimes, could I listen to you play?"

"What makes you think you're hell-bound?"

The boy was confused. "You beat me. You're better than I am."

The devil laughed. "Technically, for certain Almighty God sure. You got potential. I don't think you'll ever be better than I am, but maybe you could be."

The boy frowned, unsure. "Maybes don't count."

"The blues is about hope, boy. Under all the pain, there's hope. You played hope. You won, fair and square."

"That's bullshit."

"Not completely," the devil said. "I admit I might not have used the precise word. *Hope* is close enough, and I thought you'd know it."

"Explain it so a dumb person like me can understand."

"You're not dumb, James. Pig ignorant, yes. Dumb, no. Tell me how you feel, and I'll try to find a better word."

The boy sighed. "When you played, things made sense."

"Even your mother's pimp throwing a pot of lye in your face, leaving you piebald? That makes sense?"

"Some things don't make sense. That's one of them. So I'm too ugly—I guess that's what *piebald* means—and too stupid to even get into hell."

"*Piebald* means blotched, multicolored. You're ignorant, not dumb. I don't want to take you to hell because you don't belong there. Let me tell about hell. You sneered at 'maybes.' In hell, you've got no maybes, only might-have-beens. Nobody tortures you, there's no fire and brimstone. You go over every missed opportunity, every stupid choice, and you're locked into every one of them. You ask if you could listen to me play. I don't play in hell. I'm locked into the missed opportunities just like all the rest."

"What was your stupid choice?" the boy asked.

"None of your business," the devil said.

"You did play better'n me."

"Of course I did. I'm thousands of years older, for a start."

"Then this devil at the crossroads is just a con. You take 'em down to hell if you want to, don't if you don't want to."

"It's not that simple. Take your guitar—your very well-repaired guitar—say, 'Thank you, sir,' and go home."

"Okay," the boy said. "But can I come back? Talk to you? Maybe learn a few licks? You're about the nicest person, creature, I ever met." The boy smiled at him. "You say you can only play when you're not in hell. So it would be fun for both of us."

The devil said, "I'm not a very nice fellow. You caught me in a moment of weakness. Get along home, boy."

The boy got up and said, "Thank you, sir." He hesitated then added, "You're too hard on yourself. For pure evil, humans got devils beat by a mile."

The boy walked back down the hill, puff-puff-puff as the dust squirted under his bare feet. He disappeared into the tunnel of trees as the sun came fully up.

A Busy Day for the Bayou Banshee

Herb Shallcross

Snakes and gators slipped away unseen. A cloud of mosquitoes wreathed the swaths of Spanish moss. Hawks and owls perched stark still between kills. And far off, an ominous primeval hum haunted the night. A stone's throw from this teeming swamp, Edgar McIlhenny chawed his mouth in a show of solidarity with the horses he had tended so long. He removed a toothpick and spat in the mud, shaking his head at the rank terrain. Marcel Bettancourt stood in the doorway, scratching his head and looking over old McIlhenny. Twenty years they'd been friends, but now they looked on each other as enemies. All this because of love—Bettancourt could find no hint of sense in it.

"You don't want to come in?" Bettancourt said. "You come an awful long way to stand in the mud and talk to me in the dark."

"I didn't come to make a social call," McIlhenny said. "I think you got a pretty good idea why I come."

The two had worked together as ranch hands in East Texas before Bettancourt had crossed the border to join his extended family here in Beauregard Parish. Now McIlhenny was the proud owner of his own East Texas ranch and carried visible contempt for Bettancourt's humble home here in swamp country.

"I got some ideas," Bettancourt said. "Say, maybe your wife wants to come in and get somethin' to eat, have a chance to catch up with my lady."

"My wife is just fine where she's at."

McIlhenny's Dodge pickup idled behind him, its yellow headlamps casting a sallow glow over the swampland. The truck was big and shiny and new, everything that the low-slung Kammback behind Bettancourt was not. Mrs. Holly McIlhenny sat in the passenger seat, looking out at the men gloomily.

"Listen, Bettancourt, whatever's going on between your son and my daughter, it's gone far enough."

"Why don't you tell your daughter that?"

"Of course I've told my daughter to stay away from your boy!" McIlhenny snapped. "She's a teenage girl. She refuses to listen to reason."

"Teenage boys ain't real famous for that neither," Bettancourt said. "I'm not sure just what you expect me to do with Junior."

"*Do* with him?" McIlhenny said. "I don't care what you *do* with him! Chain him down if you have to, lock him in the cellar! Just keep him away from my little girl!"

Bettancourt hitched up his jeans and cast a level glare at his guest. Then he let his gaze fall to McIlhenny's black Lucchese boots sunk in the muck.

"I'm not at all sure I appreciate your tone, Ed," Bettancourt said.

"And I'm not at all sure I give a damn."

The two men shifted in the mud. McIlhenny stood upright in the manner he deemed befitting of a gentleman and a soldier—two identities that were identical in his way of thinking—and Bettancourt slouched with his hands in his back pockets. The pickup idled behind them with a guttural chugging that blended with the myriad croaks and caws of swamp life. The bleary yolk of the full moon swayed over the cypress trees. That ancient hum yet hung in the distance.

"Tell you what," McIlhenny said. "Bring the boy out here, and let me have a word with him, man-to-man. I'll talk some sense into him, by God."

"Junior ain't here," Bettancourt said.

"And where do you reckon he might be?"

"He never said," Bettancourt said. "Which likely means he's gone off to meet your girl someplace."

"Let's just you pray that's not the case," McIlhenny said. "Priscilla's at home with her older brother Les. I left the rifle with Les and told him that any visitors but his mama and me were to be regarded as trespassers and dealt with accordingly."

"Well, let's just you hope he's not stupid enough to listen to what you had to say," Bettancourt said. "Because Lord knows my Junior is no slouch with a pistol."

McIlhenny spat and pushed back his hat and then slapped his neck where a mosquito was feeding on him. Far to the west were storm clouds. A high-pitched wail was mounting, ricocheting through the cypress and tupelo trees. Bettancourt's eyes were big and wild, looking off toward the sound, but by and by, it subsided. The screen door swung open, and Mrs. Bettancourt poked out. She was a true Cajun matron in the old grandiose fashion, who kept her home ever filled with warmth and spice.

"You men just gonna stand out here in the dark all night staring at the mud 'r what?" she said. "I got cracklin' in here if y'all are hungry."

"I thank you, ma'am, but we haven't time to set," McIlhenny said.

"Best to get back in the house, Beatrice," Bettancourt said, but it was too late. Mrs. McIlhenny had already thrown open the door of the pickup and was rushing around the front of the truck.

"Beatrice!" she said. "So lovely to see you!"

"Holly, dawlin'! Where y'at, cher!" Beatrice Bettancourt said broadly. "Dese fools refuse to listen to reason, but why don't ya come on in and eat?"

The two women hugged, but McIlhenny pulled his wife back. The wind howled once more.

"Remember why we're here," McIlhenny said. "To separate ourselves from these people."

"Edgar!" chastised his wife.

"Separate yourselves from us?" Beatrice Bettancourt demanded. "*Sac au lait!* Ya think ya better than us now, Mr. McIlhenny?"

"It's not about what I think," McIlhenny said. "The fact is that you are *swamp people*. This is the life you chose for yourselves. I mean, your boy intends to hunt gators for a living!"

"Yeah?" Bettancourt said. "At least we don't spend our time wading through horse droppings!"

McIlhenny lunged at Bettancourt, and the two men locked hands over each other's throats. In a flash, they were rolling through the mud and, in a flash, back up on their feet. They squared off with raised fists and soiled jeans, but then both men suddenly stopped. A cloud like a cauldron was bubbling savagely in the west, driving toward them across the swampland with unbelievable speed and volition. A thin high wail whipped through the trees, rattling the very moon. The cloud swarmed purple overhead, the cry like a mad widow desperate for vengeance. The women blessed themselves; the men looked around wildly. The creatures of the swamp migrated east in a frenzied and slimy stampede.

"What on earth is it?" McIlhenny demanded. "What in God's name is wrong with this place?"

The cloud molded itself into the form of a woman cloaked in wispy rags of grey. She howled so loud that McIlhenny was forced to one knee. When he looked up, the phantom woman was looking down at him, but her face was that of his own son.

"Les?" McIlhenny said, shaken and lost. "Les, my boy, is it you?"

The apparition only howled its deafening howl, millennia of sorrow condensed in her bloodcurdling call. The phantom whipped around to face Bettancourt, who met her with wild and tear-rimmed eyes. The face he saw was that of his own son.

"Junior!" he cried. "Oh, Junior!"

The phantom woman erupted in a final spirit-shattering howl and then vanished, leaving only a fading aura like an electric current charging the air. Mrs. Bettancourt was sobbing profusely, repeating her son's name over and over in a mournful whisper—"Marcel, Marcel, Marcel."

"What the devil was that?" McIlhenny said.

Bettancourt shook his head.

"A banshee," he said, broken. "She was a banshee. Come on, we have to get back to your house."

Before McIlhenny could argue, the four of them had piled into the cab of the pickup and were roaring away toward the west, toward his home in East Texas. McIlhenny was still haunted by the banshee's wail, so much so that he could not be sure if he was only hearing the wind rushing by outside or the ghost of the wail echoing through his memory or if the woman was, in fact, still with him, sailing along with the truck and heckling them all the while.

"Banshee," McIlhenny said. "I heard of that years ago—myths and wives' tales. What the devil is it?"

Bettancourt shook his head. "A messenger. The kind you pray you never get word from."

"What are you talking about?" McIlhenny said. Mrs. Bettancourt wept on, oblivious to the discussion or the marshland rolling by outside, repeating her son's name in those doleful, woeful whispers.

"The banshee chased Irish immigrants here across the Atlantic," Bettancourt said. "The poor Irish family got run out of town, but the banshee decided to stick around and make these swamps home. Legend has it that whatever face you see on her, that person is no more."

"No more?"

"Dead," Bettancourt said.

McIlhenny was silent for a stretch. "Bull," he whispered and then stepped on the gas and sped toward home. He saw now the distance that Bettancourt's young son had traveled to meet his daughter each visit. Not much changed in the land as the miles rolled by. East Texas and the swampland weren't so different, not in any way that mattered.

They found Priscilla on the porch, still on her knees and sobbing these many hours later. On either side of her, stretched out on their backs, were her big brother Les and her love, Marcel Jr. The rifle and the pistol had been flung away in the shootout. Both young men were bloody and still.

"He would do anything for me," Priscilla whimpered. "He was the greatest man I ever knew."

Nobody was sure which dead man she was referring to, and they left it that way. The five of them hugged and wept and shook their heads as if sorrow could be shaken out like a drop of water from the ear. But the banshee's cry would not be silenced.

The Spook Light
Jay Rogers

I first heard this story from my Granny Annie in the late 1930s. The people in the story are real, and the mysterious phenomenon still appears to some who venture onto that stretch of dusty road in southwest Missouri. Ask the local folks for the directions. It's called the Hornet Spook Light. You'll know you're at the right location when, at both sides of the road, you see lots of empty beer cans.

The speedometer on Joe's new 1925 Model T Ford Tudor had marks up to forty-five miles per hour, but he knew of no reason for a human to go that fast. Once, on his journey to Neosho, Missouri, the needle on the gauge got up to twenty, but on the return to Quapaw, Oklahoma, the dark of night and rough roads kept him under twelve miles per hour. He wanted to get home before daybreak but dared not go any faster.

Joe and his wife, Annie, had recently moved from the Arkansas Ozark hills to Ottawa County, Oklahoma, where he'd been hired by one of the new diggings in the Tri-State mining region.

Joe, an experienced wagon master, and his teams of mules—hauling freight for anyone to any place—had learned to fear no man or beast on the roads. He'd built a successful business for forty-five years, and now two of his sons-in-law were among his best drivers. Within six months after relocating, Joe turned the company over to them and accepted the post of deputy sheriff when it was offered. He wanted to spend more time with his wife in their declining years.

The vehicle's lamps illuminated the dirt road, and the moonlight silhouetted the trees edging both sides of the road. Through gapes in the pines, Joe could see across the shallow ditches to the meadows and fields beyond. Civilization seemed very far away.

In the midst of this empty expanse, Joe saw something out of the ordinary. He pulled the transmission lever on the floor to its midpoint and flicked the throttle lever on the steering column up to idle speed as his foot pumped lightly on the brake pedal, bringing the Model T to a stop. His sleepiness fled; he stared across the fields with a fixed gaze.

When the event ended, he'd never felt so in need of telling someone of something he'd witnessed. He would be reluctant to admit to his dry mouth, his sweaty palms, or his hair standing on end, but what a story he had to tell!

The remainder of the trip tested the speed and reliability of his Model T. He was too busy keeping the motorcar on the road to check the speedometer.

"Annie! Wake up!" Joe shook his wife awake.

"Joe! What's the matter?" Annie sat up, startled by Joe's voice. "What time is it?"

"On the road from Neosho . . . you shoulda seen it, woman . . ."

"Seen what?" Annie slid her feet into slippers at the side of the bed and reached for her robe.

"Quit interruptin', Annie."

"Well, jes spit it out—wakin' a body from a sound sleep—I do declare."

"I seen a will-o'-the-wisp or fireball or spook light or . . . somethin' . . . out on the road from Neosho. Lordy! I had goose bumps all over, 'n' the hair on my neck stood up."

Annie turned to make her way to the kitchen. "Jes calm down, 'n' let me put the coffee on." Annie took immense pride in believing she was a voice of reason amid chaos. "Wha'ja do when you saw this here thing?"

"Uh . . . I stopped the vehicle and watched it."

"Watched it do what?" she asked while wondering why she had to pull out every thought from that man like pulling quills from a dog after he'd tangled with a porcupine.

"It jes floated out thar. 'Twas like a big, huge ball, kinda yeller-colored, 'n' then it came right dreckly at my automobile."

"How big?"

"I dunno how big it was, woman! I blinked, 'n' it was gone."

"Where'd it go?"

"Dunno. I sat there in the automobile a spell to see if it'd come back. It didn't, so I hightailed it here."

"Maybe it was the moon. Should I smell your breath?" Annie was joking, but she knew the men in the sheriff's office had a certain approach in the policy of disposing of hard evidence upon the successful disposition of a criminal bootlegging case.

"Annie . . . !"

She looked deep into his eyes to decide if he was joshing her. "All right, Joe, tell me all about this thang."

"Well, blast it! If you don't believe me, I'll drive you out there, 'n' you can see it yur own sef."

"You said it disappeared."

"It did!"

With disdain in her tone, she said, "Ain't much use a-goin' that far to see somethin' what done disappeared. You wanna sleep, or can I fix you some breakfast fore you go to work?"

Joe wasn't sleepy even though he'd not gotten a wink of sleep in the past twenty-four hours, and after breakfast, he set off about his daily business.

The foolishness was still on Annie's mind when Bertie, a neighbor lady, stepped up on the front porch and rapped at the screen door. "Mornin', Annie. I see'd y'all up early this morn. Care for company?"

"C'mon in, Bertie, coffee's still warm."

Bertie opened the screen, took off her sun bonnet, and crossed the parlor to enter Annie's kitchen.

Bertie was one of those "sees all, knows all" women, but thankfully, she didn't go about telling all . . . unless she was asked for something specific, and then even Saint Peter might pull up a chair to listen to the gossip.

"Sometimes Joe can tell a tale so windy, you'd swear the man could blow up a burlap sack."

"All men do that," said Bertie. "Zeke tol' me 'bout a man who lies so much, he had to hire a boy to call his dawg."

They giggled.

"Well . . . Joe woke me up with a story 'bout seein' a floatin' fireball out on the road toward Neosho."

"Why, fiddledeedee," exclaimed Bertie. "That weren't no fib. Folks round here don't bother talkin' on it les'un somebody just happens to see it again."

Annie sat her cup down and leaned forward. "You seen this?"

"No, not my own personal sef, but there's plenty a folks round here what can attest to it. I don't know much, but't ain't no fib."

Annie picked up her cup and rubbed at the wet ring it left on the bare oak tabletop. "I recall listenin' to some ol' folks back home spinnin' yarns 'bout fireballs a-dwellin' 'n' a-flittin' round in swamps, but I figured that was jes fer entertainin' the younguns."

Bertie nodded and said, "I guess you 'n' me ain't lived here long enough to heer ev'thing."

That disclosure surprised Annie. Bertie was the town's midwife, and her husband Zeke was the carpenter, who built cabinets and coffins for the community. Bertie was fond of saying, "B'twixt Zeke 'n' me, us two see 'em a-comin' 'n' a-goin'."

Bertie said, "Ol' Miz Lucy would know 'bout such things."

Annie raised her eyebrows. "Who?"

"Miz Lucy. In her seventy years a-livin' here 'n' bein' a Quapaw Injun 'n' all, thar ain't much she don't know 'bout this neck o' the woods."

"Ain't never met her."

Bertie rose from her chair. "I ain't seen Miz Lucy in a coon's age. Let's go a-callin' 'n' see how the ol' soul's a-feelin' these days. She tell you 'bout ev'thing."

The two women set off on a mission of discovery. They left their coffee cups sitting on the table and started toward ol' Miz Lucy's shack at the edge of town.

That evening, as supper was being set, Annie apologized to Joe for doubting his word that morning, and she told him of her visit with ol' Miz Lucy.

"Ol' Miz Lucy say them lights been seen many times by many a fine, upstanding citizen and Injuns too since b'fore the Jayhawker wars."

As Joe waited for Annie to be seated to say grace, he thought, *It ain't often Annie admits she was wrong. I'd best stay quiet and let her run down.*

"She say there's a tale o' two Quapaw Indian lovers bein' chased by their tribe's warrior braves 'n' an angry father." Annie set a bowl on the table and settled into her chair. "Bertie 'n' me picked them greens comin' away from Miz Lucy's."

Joe clasped Annie's hand, lowered his eyes, and said, "Bless us 'n' the grub." He tucked a napkin in his collar and continued, "Pass them mashed taters, please. What happened to them kids?"

"That lovin' pair got cornered on a high cliff 'n' jumped off, smack-dab in the Spring River."

"Pass me them biscuits, Annie. I suppose the fall kilt 'em . . . mayhaps they drown."

"Well, you supposed right, Joe. Miz Lucy, she say, that there spook light is speculated to be one of the younguns walkin' round a-lookin' for t'other."

Annie's recounting of the tale caused her mind to wander on things of feminine romanticizing, and she grew silent.

Joe figured she'd finally run down. "I talked to some ol' timers round town, 'n' they told me a few things." He reached for the last soda biscuit. "Is there any more red-eye gravy?"

Annie shook off her reverie and said, "A few things about what? They's a little bit left 'n' more in the skillet . . . a few things about what?"

Joe's face broke out in a knowing grin. "I heered it's the ghost of a miner searchin' for his ol' lady 'n' kids, what got kidnapped by a band of renegade Indians way back, long time ago."

Annie was a bit miffed. "Couldn't be a miner. T'weren't no mines here b'fore the Northern Aggression. I reckon that ol' Injun woman knows better."

Joe could hardly conceal his grin as he said, "And nother feller claimed the light is caused by the devil himself. He said that if a certain bridge out there is crossed a certain number of times, the devil himself will pop up in a cloud of smoke."

"T'weren't no bridges back then neither." Hearing about the devil making an appearance anywhere at any time was something Annie would never take lightly, and Joe's grin split his face as Annie saw he was now teasing her.

Using the last biscuit to sop up the last spots of red-eye gravy on his plate, Joe said, "Well . . . no matter what it was that I seen, there's just no denyin' I did see it."

Annie wondered how a tale could take on so many reasons for being. "Joe. I've got a hankerin' to see those great balls of fire or whatever with my very own eyes."

Joe said, "'Twas a sight to behold."

"Ain't never seen a real live ghost. Don't think one 'd pose much more danger than a wampus cat."

"Probably not," said Joe. "You get a chance to make an apple pie today?"

Annie was committed. "And if it turns out to be the devil— why, Lordy, I'll carry along the Good Book, 'n' that'll pertect us. Such a tale that'd make at church next Sunday. Berry pie's all I got."

Over the next couple of weeks, Joe and Annie found the time to make two trips to the dusty country road late at night. Their destination was about twenty miles east of their home, just a shade less than a two-hour drive, one way in those days.

They returned home disappointed both times. Annie said she didn't cotton much to losing sleep over a silly spook light, but she was determined to catch a glimpse of it, so they planned another midnight drive.

It was a typical fall evening, warm in the day but cooling off as the sun set. The chill night air and a gentle breeze produced wisps of fog that drifted above the meadows. The rustler's moon gave just enough light to make out the shapes of trees to either side of the gravel road.

They traveled eastward over the stretch of road where Joe had seen the spook light. At a wide place, they turned the Model T around, drove back about four miles, and made another U-turn. They recalled the story that if a certain bridge were crossed a certain number of times, the devil would appear. There was a bridge over a small creek in the middle of the four-mile stretch they'd been driving, and not knowing which bridge was the "certain bridge" nor being sure of the "certain number," they reasoned that since the devil's number is 666, they should steer clear of the number six. Two round-trips meant they'd cross the bridge four times, so it was agreed that making two round-trips was the prudent thing to do.

On the second circuit that night, they'd crossed the bridge for the third time and were about a mile from the east turn-around place when Joe pulled the transmission lever on the floor to its midpoint, pushed the throttle lever on the steering column up to idle speed, pumped the brake pedal, and turned off the headlights. The vehicle slid to a stop in the darkness.

"Over yonder," he whispered, "look to the left, through the trees 'n' across that field. There's a creek running through there, 'n' I see a light a-followin' the creek bed."

Joe opened the door. He stood on the running board and reached for the twelve-gauge double-barreled scattergun he kept beneath the driver's seat. He felt for the bulge of his .38 Smith & Wesson revolver in his coat pocket . . . just in case it was needed.

"Stay put in the car, Annie," he said. "I don't want you a-running loose in the wilderness."

"What are you doin', Joe?"

"If it's a human out thar, I wanna know who it is."

"And if it ain't human?"

Joe tuned to Annie, lifted the right lapel of his coat, revealing his badge, and said, "Well then, I'll jes flash my lawman's shield 'n' impress it into leavin' peaceful-like."

"Joe," she whispered. "Don't shoot it. It might be a farmer a-looking for a stray out there."

"I ain't a-goin' to shoot the gol' blasted thing les'un it shoots first. And it ain't no man. It's too high off the ground to be a lantern."

Annie often said, "I don't skeer easy—'cept 'bout snakes, but I do git concerned." And being concerned, she had no intention of sitting within the confines of anything. She quietly opened her door and stepped to the ground. She felt for the bulge of her Bible in her apron pocket . . . just in case it was needed.

Annie tiptoed softly to the front of the car. She could see the light moving down the middle of the field. Sometimes it swayed from side to side, and once in a while, it would bounce up and down like a cork bobber, down at the pond, when a fish latched hold of the bait.

Joe stood near the driver's side of the car with the scatter-gun in his left hand, muzzle pointed skyward. "It's a-moseyin' along right close to the creek bed. 'Bout the same pace as a man on the trot."

"Maybe it'll just keep a-goin' where it's headed," Annie whispered.

"I don't think so, Annie. It's makin' a turn 'n' comin' this way."

Annie watched the light perform a wide turn. Her concern increased, and as she also often said, "When I'm gettin' a mite concerned, I think of the scriptures . . . and if'n the stress don't fade, I start a-singing church hymns." She was contemplating an appropriate scripture.

"Lookit, Annie! The blame thing's a-makin' a beeline dreck-ly at us!"

The glowing orb was now thirty yards from the road. "Stop! I'm a deputy lawman, 'n' I'm a-sayin' stop!"

"I don't believe you impressed it, Joe."

Seeing the light coming straight at her, Annie forgot about a scripture and began mulling over a hymn appropriate to the occasion. The only hymns she could bring to mind were "Bringing in the Sheaves" and "This Little Light of Mine." The latter seemed a tad improper, so she began singing the former.

She finished the first four words of the hymn as Joe reached for the bulge in his coat pocket and yelled out, "Halt! Halt or I'll shoot!"

The light didn't halt.

Joe raised the pistol in the air and fired off two rounds while Annie sang the second line of the hymn. "Bringing—*bang*—in the—*bang*—sheaves . . ."

The light didn't halt.

Annie yelled, "Joe! Let's git in this motorcar!" But instead of moving, she began singing again, this time with a slight tremor in her voice and definitely at a higher octave. "We will come rejoicing, bringing in the sheaves."

The light was now less than twenty yards away from the road.

Joe slipped the revolver back into his coat pocket and raised the scattergun. "I've got two barrels of double-aught buckshot aimed your way! Now stop!"

The glowing orb was approaching the shallow ditch next to the gravel road.

"Joe! Get in this here motorcar right now!" Annie screamed as she pulled the Book of Testaments from her apron pocket and held it aloft.

Joe aimed his sawed-off shotgun, firing directly at the light—*ka-boom*. Annie, holding the book aloft, yelled, "Depart from us, ye that work iniquity, Matthew 7 somethin'!" Joe pulled the second trigger—*ka-boom*.

The echoes of the ruckus faded away.

Joe and Annie blinked their eyes. The light had disappeared.

Joe stood next to the open driver's side door of the motorcar. Annie stood to his right. They noticed the crisp night air and the soft breeze. They were aware of the rustler's moon giving just enough light to make out the shapes of the trees to either side of the gravel road.

Then they walked around the automobile, looking in and over and under the vehicle. They saw nothing unusual.

The only sound was the motorcar still idling.

Annie took up her place in the passenger's seat. Joe walked slowly around the car again, then stepped up on the running board and slid into the driver's seat.

Finally, Annie broke the quiet. In a small voice, she sang, "What a friend we have in Jesus, all our sins and griefs to bear." Her voice became stronger and more confident. "What a privilege to carry everything to God in prayer!"

By the third line of the hymn, she was sounding as if she were singing solo at a tent revival meeting of deaf Baptists. "O what peace we often forfeit, O what needless pain we bear, All because we do not carry everything to God in prayer."

Joe eased the throttle lever on the steering column down, turned on the headlights, and started homeward down the dusty country road, crossing the bridge for the fourth time.

On the last note of her song, Joe looked at Annie and said with a chuckle, "Now weren't that somethin' to behold? I don't know which did the trick, the double-aught buckshot or Matthew 7 somethin'."

Annie didn't say anything. She kept singing more hymns, and Joe joined in with her. "Rock of Ages," "Shall We Gather at the River?," "Just a Closer Walk with Thee."

As they neared the town of Quapaw, their singing was now clamorous, and the houses were dark.

Joe and Annie didn't give a damn about waking folks. They continued singing . . . all the way home.

That Damned Game

Kristina R. Mosley

G ravel popped under tires. Lily Duncan grabbed her brown coat from the wooden rack by the door. She put it on over her blue knee-length dress and pulled her long silver braid out from the collar. A car door shut outside, followed by crunching on the driveway and then footsteps on the porch.

The woman opened her door before her visitor could knock. The thin frame of Pauline Dobson stood before her on the porch. A pink floral shirt peeked out from her red wool coat, and a black beret covered her curly dyed-brown hair.

"So you ready to go?" Lily asked.

"It's nice to see you too," Pauline replied.

Lily hobbled down the wooden steps, her cane tapping. She ambled across the dead grass and entered the passenger side of Pauline's powder blue car.

"Thanks for picking me up," Lily said. "I'd drive, but you know how my nerves get me."

Her companion sighed as she pulled out of the driveway. "Don't pretend it's your 'nerves.' Everyone in town knows you got your license suspended because you had too many speeding tickets."

"Well, my nerves made me hit the accelerator so hard."

The old women were quiet as the car moved down the road, away from town.

"Are we playing at the church or the lodge today?" Lily asked finally.

"Neither, actually. Helen Crosby told me about this new place."

"Really? Where is it?"

"It's down towards Taylorsville. Helen's never been there, but it'd be a good change of pace, wouldn't it? We could see new places, meet new people."

Lily didn't reply. She didn't like the idea of going somewhere new. The lodge and the church were familiar. *You're being unreasonable, though*, Lily told herself. *Let Pauline go to the new place.*

"What's wrong, Lily?" her friend asked. "You're being awfully quiet."

"I was just thinking about how I'm too stuck in my ways."

"Oh," Pauline replied quietly. A few moments later, she turned left, guiding the vehicle down a bumpy dirt road lined with trees.

"Where is this place?" Lily asked.

Pauline scanned the horizon. "Helen said it was a few miles down this road." The woods grew darker the further the car went. She flicked on the headlights.

"The bingo hall is this way?" Lily asked.

"I guess," the driver muttered quietly. The car's headlights shone on a cluster of trees at the end of the road.

"It's a dead end," Lily said.

Pauline didn't respond, continuing to drive toward the trees.

"Are you trying to get us killed?" Lily shouted.

Pauline stomped on her brakes. "There it is," she said, pointing to her right.

Lily's eyes widened as she saw a small red brick building. "You sure this is the right place? I don't see any cars."

Pauline pulled into the parking lot, which was little more than a patch of bare dirt. She pointed to a sign that had the words "Seniors' Bingo, Feb. 20, 1:30 pm" stenciled in black paint. She looked at her watch. "It's 1:25." She shut off the car and got out.

Lily remained in the passenger seat, staring at the building. A feeling of dread tightened in her chest. *Something's wrong here*, she thought.

"Are you coming?"

"Yeah," Lily said shakily. She got out of the car and limped to the door where Pauline already stood.

They entered a well-lit cream-colored hallway. Amber light fixtures cast a golden glow on the walls and the white tile floor.

"Well, this is nice," Pauline said.

Lily nodded. "It's a lot nicer than any place I've played bingo in before."

"I wonder where we're supposed to go."

The women walked around, trying to find another person. Pauline stopped to admire a large landscape painting, while Lily looked into a big mirror with a gold-painted frame. The soft lighting concealed the old woman's wrinkles, making her appear decades younger.

"I need to take this mirror home with me."

Someone chuckled behind her. *That wasn't Pauline*, she realized. A man's reflection peered back at her from the mirror. She turned around, clutching her chest.

"You almost scared the life out of me!"

The man smiled. He was blond and looked no older than thirty. His red dress shirt was open at the collar. "My apologies."

Pauline stood next to her friend.

"Good afternoon, ladies. Are y'all here to play bingo?" he asked.

Lily didn't hear a familiar twang on the word *y'all*. She didn't think the man was from the area.

"Yes, we are," Pauline replied, stepping forward.

"Great!" he exclaimed. "Nice to meet both of you. I'm Eric, and if you follow me, we're just about to start." He walked off, and Pauline immediately followed.

"'We'? There are other people here?" Lily asked. She struggled to catch up with Pauline and Eric.

"Yes, there are," Eric replied, turning slightly. "Everyone's waiting to begin."

"Well then, where are everybody's cars?"

He didn't answer. Instead, he turned left into a doorway. The two women followed.

Lily looked around the rose pink room. About twenty women, anywhere in age from sixty to eighty, sat at long wooden tables, bingo cards in front of them. She didn't recognize any of the women, which she thought was odd. She assumed she had met everyone in town over her eighty years. *Well, we are closer to Taylorsville*, she remembered. *Surely, I don't know everyone there.*

A small woman jumped in her path. She looked younger than the others. She wore her brown hair in a messy bob that rested against her receding chin. Large teeth protruded from her mouth. The woman's beady black eyes darted from Lily to Pauline.

"Hello," she squeaked nervously. "Would you like something to drink? We have coffee, tea, hot cocoa . . ."

"No, thanks," Lily replied. "I don't want to risk spilling something on my cards."

"I'll take some cocoa," Pauline answered.

The ratlike woman poked her hands from the sleeves of her brown cardigan and poured a hot liquid from a carafe into a foam cup. She handed it to Pauline.

"Oh!" Lily's companion said enthusiastically. "It has miniature marshmallows." She sipped carefully.

Lily and Pauline took the only two empty seats that were next to each other. Bingo cards waited for them on the table.

Eric walked over to a wooden podium. Beside him on a table sat a squirrel cage with colorful plastic balls inside. The rat woman stood next to him, ready to turn the handle. "Thank you for coming today," he said. "Are y'all ready to play some bingo?"

The women in the room murmured.

"All right then," Eric said with a smile. "Let's get started."

The first prize the women played for was a gaudy green ring. Lily didn't care if she won or lost. The women continued playing for trinkets, and the winners were delighted with their prizes.

Five games had passed, and neither Lily nor Pauline had won anything. Lily leaned over and whispered in her friend's ear. "I don't know about this. Everyone else is winning."

"I noticed," Pauline replied. "I was thinking about leaving after this game." She took a long drink from her cup.

Lily turned back to the front. The rat woman stared at her. She said something to Eric, and he nodded. When the game ended, Lily and Pauline both stood up.

"Now," Eric said, "we're going to raise the stakes a bit." The rat woman slid a white envelope to him. He held it up. "In this envelope is a gift certificate for fifty dollars in free groceries."

Lily and Pauline both sat down.

Eric started calling numbers, and soon, Lily made a diagonal line on her card. "Bingo!" she called. She collected her prize and stuck it in her purse. Then everyone played for a crystal bell, bells being one of Pauline's special favorites. She won it.

Afterward, Lily and Pauline won alternating games, each time getting something they enjoyed. Lily won a travel-sized photo album, perfect for carrying pictures of her grandchildren, and a pink carrying case filled with crochet hooks. Pauline collected a porcelain parrot that resembled her late bird, Reynaldo, and a white silk fan with a cherry blossom tree painted on it.

Lily became suspicious. "Something's wrong, Pauline. We keep winning."

"So? It's about time our luck changed."

"My luck's not that good, though."

Another game started, but Lily didn't pay much attention. Instead, she noticed the way the other women looked at Eric. There was a strange gleam in their eyes, something like lust. She glanced at Pauline. The same look was in her eyes. *That's not right*, Lily thought. *Pauline Dobson is the most prudish person I know.*

She turned her attention to Eric. He had a big smile on his face. She looked back at the women in the room. *They should be ashamed of themselves*, she thought. *He's young enough to be their grandson. Why are they acting like this?*

Lily saw that everyone else had a foam cup sitting in front of them. *There must be something in the drinks*, she realized. She knocked over Pauline's cup.

"Why did you do that!" her friend shouted.

"It's drugged."

"But . . . miniature marshmallows," she said.

The rat woman appeared, as if out of thin air, with a new foam cup. She set it on the table. "I have a fresh cup of cocoa for you, Mrs. Dobson."

Pauline smiled and sipped. "Thank you."

How did she know Pauline's name? Lily wondered. "Something isn't right about this place. I'm leaving." She stood up, her chair screeching across the tile floor. She picked up her purse and headed toward the door. Pauline didn't follow.

She left the room and turned down the hallway. Eric stood in front of her.

"How are you here?" she asked. "You're calling the bingo game."

A shadow passed over his blue eyes. There was something ancient there, something far older than what Lily saw when she looked in the mirror every day. "Mysterious ways," he replied with a grin.

The old woman gasped. "You are not the Lord."

"Well, no . . ."

"You must be the devil."

"I'm not him either. I'm just someone who gives people what they want."

"Well, I want to leave," she replied. She pushed past him.

"But why, Lily?" Eric asked. "Aren't you having fun?"

"It isn't fun to win all the time."

He looked back at Pauline. She concentrated on her card with a slight smile on her face. "Your friend seems to be enjoying herself."

"She doesn't know what's going on."

"And you do?" he asked coldly. He stood close to her, his body blocking the light.

She gasped but tried not to let her surprise show. "Not completely, but it's not right."

"I'm giving you decrepit old women some happiness in your sad last days. How isn't that right?"

All fear left Lily at that moment, anger replacing it. She lifted her cane and hit Eric in the shin. "How dare you call me 'decrepit'!" She continued to beat the man.

He put up his arms to shield his head. "Fine!" he screamed. "If you want to leave so badly, go!" The building seemed to shake with his words.

Lily hobbled as quickly as she could down the hallway. She was almost to the door and looked back. Eric was closer. She yelped and tried to quicken her pace. She pushed through the door and entered the cold winter air.

Darkness greeted her.

Oh Lord, I'm blind! she thought. She blinked a few times, and her eyes slowly adjusted. "How could it be nighttime?" she muttered as she walked. "It was only 1:30 when we got here. We weren't in the building that long, surely."

The frigid air cut through Lily's clothes, biting at her arthritic joints. She wished she'd taken Pauline's keys, suspended license be damned. The cold would hurt her, and she didn't know how to hotwire a car. She looked back at the bingo hall and contemplated going inside. *No,* she thought. *I might not make it out again.*

She crunched unsteadily on the gravel. Pauline's car was nowhere in sight. "They must've hidden it," she said aloud. "I need to get some help." She hobbled out of the parking lot and onto the dirt road. Her body ached with each bump in the road's uneven surface, but she pressed on.

The road was completely dark. The wind blew viciously, chilling her to the bone. She thought she heard noises in the trees on either side of her. She didn't know if they were from normal night creatures or from worse things.

"Help," she prayed.

Lily limped down the desolate road for what seemed like hours. She noticed something moving out of the corner of her eye. When she looked up, she saw two bright lights shining on the trees in front of her. She walked faster, thinking it was Eric trying to catch up to her. The lights grew brighter, and she jumped into the roadside brush to escape.

"Ma'am, what are you doin'?" a man's voice asked. It wasn't Eric.

Lily peeked out from her hiding place. A county police car was idling on the road. The driver, a man with greying hair and a plump face, had rolled down the window.

She emerged from bushes. "I-I was walking," she said nervously.

"Where you walkin' at this time of night?"

"I was trying to find help. My friend is trapped in a bingo hall."

The police officer raised his eyebrows. "But ma'am, there ain't no bingo halls out here, just woods."

"I was just there!" Lily shouted, waving her cane above her head.

The driver's side door opened, and the cop pulled himself, grunting, out of the car. He waddled over to the woman. He was barely taller than she was. According to his nameplate, he was Deputy Yates.

"Ma'am, please calm down. I'll take you home, maybe call a relative for you." He put a hand on her arm, but she knocked it away.

"We don't have time for that. Pauline's in danger." She pulled open the door and sat in the front seat. "I'm going to show you where the bingo hall is since you obviously don't know."

He sighed and got in the driver's seat. The front of the car sank considerably. "Fine. Then I'm takin' you home." He started the car.

"It was that way," she said, pointing behind her.

Yates made a U-turn and sped away. Lily peered through the windshield, searching for the building's dirt driveway. She couldn't find it.

The car screeched to a halt. Lily put her hand against the dashboard to keep herself from flying out of the seat. "What did you do that for?" she screeched.

The cop pointed. "The road's a dead end."

"It was right here." She got out of the car and started walking. She tried to remember how far the car was from the dead end when Pauline turned. That spot was nothing but trees now. "It was here, I swear," she said softly.

"Are you sure 'bout that, Mrs. Duncan? I ain't sayin' you're lyin', but maybe you dreamed it up. Maybe it was some kind of . . . delusion or somethin'. You are kinda up in years."

Lily smacked the police officer in the knee with her cane. "I may be old, but my mind's still as sharp as a tack."

Yates tried to shake the pain out of his leg. "Well, your aim's good anyway."

"I just don't know what happened to Pauline."

"You know what? I bet she'll turn up. We can't do anything 'bout a missin' adult before twenty-four hours, but I'll make sure someone goes by her house tomorrow."

Lily didn't like the idea of not looking for Pauline, but she didn't know what else to do. Plus she was tired, her bones hurt, and she had medicine to take. "I suppose that's all we can do."

"You can call the sheriff's office tomorrow to check." He guided Lily to the car. "Now where do you live?"

They drove in silence until Yates pulled up in front of Lily's home.

"Now you have a good night. Don't worry about your friend. She'll be fine."

"If you say so."

Lily saw the bingo hall again in her dreams. Rows of desiccated women sat at long tables, daubers in their hands. The rat woman gnawed on a fragile femur. Eric stood above them, still spinning the squirrel cage. He glared at Lily, his red eyes flashing.

"Pauline won't remember," he snarled. "No one will believe you."

♣

The first thing she did when she got up the next morning was call the sheriff's office. A male officer answered.

"A deputy named Yates told me to call this morning regarding my friend, Pauline Dobson."

"Yes, ma'am. He left a note."

"Did you find her?"

"We did. An officer went by her house this morning. She was just fine."

Lily's jaw dropped. "How did she get away from the bingo hall?"

The police officer on the other end was quiet for a few moments. "Mrs. Dobson said that she didn't go to any bingo hall yesterday."

"What?"

"She said that she didn't even see you yesterday."

"But she did," Lily exclaimed.

"I'm sorry, ma'am. That's just what she told the officer."

Pauline won't remember. She sighed. "I know. Thank you."

"You're welcome. Do you have any other questions?"

"I have a hell of a lot of questions, but you can't answer them."

Lily hung up and sat in her silent living room. How could Pauline not remember what happened? She wasn't usually forgetful. Did the thing that made her and the other women googly-eyed at Eric block her memory too?

The woman picked up the telephone. "Maybe I could jog her memory," she murmured. She dialed the number, and after a few rings, a familiar voice answered.

"It's so good to hear your voice," Lily said.

"It's good to hear yours too," Pauline replied, her tone questioning.

"So the police went by your house today."

"They did. What was that all about?"

"You don't remember?"

"Remember what? He asked me about some bingo hall, but I didn't go to the church or the lodge yesterday. I didn't go *anywhere* yesterday. I didn't see anyone."

"But what about Eric? The rat woman? They put something in your cocoa, and you looked at the man inappropriately."

"I would do no such th—"

"Miniature marshmallows!"

"I think you made this up," Pauline said sternly.

"I didn't," Lily protested.

"I'm not saying you did it to stir up trouble or anything. Maybe you dozed off while watching TV."

Yesterday's events started to become foggy in Lily's mind, as if she didn't live them. They were like an old story someone had told her years earlier. *No.* She shook her head. The previous day's events happened even if no one else remembered. She knew she had to play along, though, because she didn't want anyone to think she was crazy.

"Maybe that's what happened," she said.

Pauline was quiet for a few moments. "Do you need to go to the store?" she asked finally.

"Yeah, I do."

"I'm heading that way after my stories go off. I'll see you in about an hour."

Lily hung up the phone and stared at the soap opera coming on the television. "That's it!" she yelled. Her purse sat on the kitchen table. She dumped its contents, searching for the gift certificate from the grocery store. "It'll prove I'm not crazy."

She shuffled through the pile of candy wrappers and old receipts, but she couldn't find what she was looking for. "But I stuck it in my purse yesterday," she lamented.

What if you didn't? a voice in her head countered. It was a man's voice.

She shoved the things back into her purse and walked back to the living room.

"No one will believe you," a man's voice said.

She turned to the TV and saw a blond man on the screen. He had the same blue eyes, the same smug smile that Eric had. She gasped. The camera panned out, showing him talking to a red-haired woman. She sighed and sat back in her chair.

Lily stared at the television but couldn't concentrate on the soap opera. She wondered if she was losing her mind. She was eighty after all. Maybe she wasn't as sharp as she used to be.

She sat there, thinking, when a car honked outside. The soap opera on TV was off, so she assumed Pauline was there for her. She grabbed her purse as quickly as she could, put on her coat, and walked out to Pauline's car.

"Why didn't you come to the door?" Lily asked, closing the door. She buckled her seat belt.

"It's cold. I figured you'd hear me."

Lily didn't reply. Neither woman spoke while they traveled to the grocery store. Pauline didn't ask about the bingo hall, and Lily wanted to pretend it didn't happen.

Her eyes drifted to the side of the street. A blond man walked down the sidewalk, a red shirt poking out of his black leather jacket. He stared right at her and smiled. She gasped. It

THE OLD WEIRD SOUTH

was Eric. Speechless, she pulled on Pauline's sleeve just as her friend steered the car left.

"What is it?" she snapped. "You're going to make me have an accident."

Lily pointed to where Eric was. "It's the man from the bingo hall. Maybe you'll remember if you see him."

"You're still talking about that?" Pauline looked in the rear-view mirror. "No one's there."

Lily peered into the side mirror. No one was on the sidewalk. She strained to turn around in her seat, unbuckling her seat belt to move more freely. Eric had vanished.

"You didn't see anyone, did you?"

Lily kept her eyes on the floorboard. "No, I didn't."

"I hate to say this, especially given how you are," Pauline began. "I'm not trying to be mean, but maybe it's all in your head." She pulled the car into the grocery store parking lot.

Lily looked up at the car's reflection in the store's plate glass windows. "Maybe, maybe not," she whispered.

Tennessee Ghosts

Stephen Newton

In the mid-1970s, I lived for a time in the former home of Stringbean, one of the Grand Ole Opry's longest running stars. Stringbean was an old-time baggy pants comedian and frailing-style banjo player. On November 11, 1973, two local hilltop thugs broke into Stringbean's house. They sat in the dark smoking cigarettes and drinking beer, waiting for the old scarecrowlike country star, returning home after a performance at the Opry, to come up the driveway that crossed the creek at the end of the hollow, where the freight trains roared around the bend and shook the walls.

They met Stringbean and struggled just inside the front door, and the two young toughs dragged the fifty-eight-year-old man to the floor and shot him in the chest, killing him. His wife, Estelle, ran out into the yard. They shot her in the back of the head and left her corpse lying in the gravel driveway. Grandpa Jones, the star of the *Hee Haw* television show, found the bodies the next morning when he came to get Stringbean to go fishing. Rumor had it that Stringbean was rich but cheap and that he had a fortune stashed in his little house. He did have his earnings from the Opry that night in a secret pocket in his bib overalls, but the killers, as stupid as they were murderous, did not find the money.

I lived in this house in the winter of 1978, five years after the murders. At that time, there were still bloodstains under the throw rug in the living room and bullet holes in the front doorjamb. There was a cave a stone's throw from the back door, the entrance set into the steep, rocky hardwood hillside of the hollow. The Akemans—Stringbean's real name was David

Akeman—had mortared fieldstones around a silver freezer door in the mouth of the dark hole.

Gethsemane. Silver and stone. Moonlight on leaves.

Hanging in the cool darkness inside the cave were heavy stainless steel meat hooks, slaughterhouse weight. The temperature was perfect for curing meat. The Akemans used the cave to hang country hams, but long after they were dead and gone, the silver hooks still hung in the dark.

Around the shoulder of the hill out back was a clapboard house with wraparound porches and an old weathered barn. I vaguely knew the young man who lived there—he was frequently getting drunk, wrecking motorcycles, fighting, getting arrested. Years before, legend had it that his grandfather had bought an old Wurlitzer jukebox, which he kept out in the barn. So far as anyone knew, he had never plugged it in and played any music. One day, the old man walked out to the barn, plugged in his jukebox, turned it on full blast, and hung himself.

When they cut him down, they supposedly left the rest of the rope hanging. It was reportedly still there dangling—frayed, pale in the gloom—when I lived around the corner of the hill. I wondered what song he played when he hung himself, but I never walked back to the barn to see if the frayed rope still hung from the rafters.

Railroad tracks ran along the side of the mountain across the hollow. For years, locals had talked about seeing the lights of a phantom brakeman on this exact stretch of rail. They would go out on the tracks in the dark humid stillness, and a swinging lantern-sized glow would appear, waist-high. If one came too close, the light would disappear and then reappear immediately behind the intruder. It was what local teenagers did for fun—go out to the hollow, walk the tracks, and watch for the swaying light.

I was friends with a young married couple who were renting Stringbean's little death-house. It was a tiny four-room red cottage at the end of a long gravel drive, shaded by tall old maples. They had a vacant unheated room off the back porch where I stayed for most of that winter, only a few feet from the sealed silver mouth of the meat-hook cave.

My friends had heard what sounded like footsteps on the roof at night. Once, a latched back door flew open, and their dogs went frantic, barking and snarling into the maw of the void. Shit happens, as the T-shirts and bumper stickers tell us; but back in the "Holler Where the Sun Don't Shine," as one local wag termed it, or "Dead Man's Holler," as another called it, it seemed to be concentrated, focused, channeled.

This was a kind of unclean monkey business, however, to be even distantly associated with the sanctified, sanitized monument to gingham Main Street that is the Grand Ole Opry. Tourists come to Nashville to escape, and as much as they love drama and tension, they still want the heavens to open with redemption at the denouement. Perhaps the South knows gothic all too well, and Southerners don't want it in their entertainment.

Maybe they just don't want it on vacation, which is entirely possible, but it also could be that this is an example of the kind of thinking that gives rise to the gothic in the first place—that is, that the denial and repression of the shadowy side makes it amplify and energize and morph, precisely because these primal energies have been forbidden. The imp of the perverse may be trapped for the short term, but it always finds some way to escape.

In Dead Man's Holler, these twisted forces seemed to have gone to otherworldly, even demonic, extremes, a hell-bound train from Memphis or New Orleans or Montgomery or Nashville that roared through the Dixie night, spraying pestilence and horror in its wake.

I've never known one way or the other if I was imagining things back in the Hollow Where the Sun Don't Shine, but I can say for sure that thirty-four years later, it still feels like I had a brief glimpse into a side of the South that I had only read about.

It's nothing more than that. It's just a feeling.

It's a feeling, however, that still gives me a chill to think about, when I picture the silver door of the cave in the moonlight, in back of the little house where the Opry star and his wife were murdered. I can still hear the sound of the train rattling through the hollow, and I remember the way that I pictured the engineer being a skeleton in an engineer's cap, balling the jack on his hell-bound train.

The Gift of Understanding

Sherry Fasano

My family's not superstitious. Not really. We're Baptists from way back, and everybody knows Baptists don't believe in such; but my Grandmama Minnie's people were from the low country of South Carolina, and they believed there were some things that couldn't be explained, and it was best not to try. She attached certain meanings to everyday happenings that made no sense. When a bird flew into the window and broke its neck, she exclaimed, "Lord, have mercy, children, you know what that means." A dog howling when church bells rang was even more ominous. None of the women in the family thought it wise to sweep sand out of the house when it was raining; and her mother, Granny Cribb, saw visions and declared whenever she heard ringing in her ears that it was a "death bell," and sure enough, somebody died shortly thereafter. They all stayed indoors during the month of August—dog days. Mad dogs roamed the countryside, and sores didn't heal. Sadly, these gifts have been slipping away with each new generation, but Mama still remembers one strange occurrence and vows it's true. It happened when she was a little girl in the 1930s. The story was retold for years on Grandmama's front porch, when summer darkness settled in and whippoorwills began calling.

Grandmama Minnie and Granddaddy Clarence sold their house in town and bought property adjoining that of Minnie's sister, Sarah Jane, and her husband, Spurgeon, when Mama was a little girl. The property was old farmland and had a frame house with no electricity or indoor plumbing, but Minnie was expecting again, and because her mother lived with Sarah Jane, she was overjoyed to be near family. With quite a few acres, Clarence could farm some and supplement his growing family's table with game.

The property was remote and only accessible by a narrow dirt road winding several miles off the highway. Few visitors came to call; most were family. The folks from Conway came once in a while and usually traveled by bus. Their visits were preceded by a letter to let the family in Columbia know when they would be arriving and was posted weeks in advance in case it wasn't convenient. Since the closest bus stop was out on the highway, Clarence and Spurgeon drove out on the day promised and gathered them up. Mama said they were always thrilled when aunts and uncles paid a visit, and it was a special treat when cousins came along. Preparations included a thorough house cleaning with the airing out of mattresses and rugs and a scrubbing down of the outhouse. Times were hard, but Minnie and Sarah Jane shared groceries and cooked together for days. Breads and jelly cakes were baked, and Mama and her cousins were sent out to the edge of the woods to pick wild blackberries for cobblers. The sisters each sacrificed fat hens from their yards to fry up crispy brown or bake with cornbread dressing. Clarence gathered whatever could be used from the garden, and Spurgeon provided game. The whole time cooking was going on in the kitchen, family stories were being told. Children weren't usually privy to family gossip, but if they hid under the table and kept quiet, they could pick up all sorts of tidbits. They learned which aunts dipped snuff on the sly and who was in the family way again. The occasional recounting of sickness and death was whispered in hushed tones. One incident was remembered over and over, and as I said, my mama witnessed it.

Sarah Jane worked a night shift job over at Camp Jackson, and one afternoon, she was getting ready for work in her big front bedroom while giving her daughter instructions for the younger children. Standing in front of the mirror combing her hair, she saw the reflection of the huge oak out in the front yard, and there was a man sitting up against the trunk. As she turned around to look, she recognized his face and grabbed her daughter's hand. "Lord, Bobby, it's Uncle Richard. He's come to visit without letting us know and walked all the way out from the highway. Let's go help him in. He must be exhausted!" Excited, Bobby jumped off the bed and followed her mother through the living room and out the front door. When they got out to the front porch, no one was under the tree or anywhere else in the yard.

Minnie was sweeping the front porch and Mama and her sisters were playing on the steps when Sarah Jane pulled her big sedan into the driveway a short while later.

Before Sarah Jane got to the porch, she called out, "You younguns run play. I need to talk to your mother." All the children scattered, except for Mama, who quietly kept her place on the steps.

"Minnie, something bad's gonna happen down in Conway. If you get word this evening, send somebody to let me know." She recounted her vision, and they grabbed each other's hands and hugged.

Minnie was tense all evening, hurrying supper and putting the children to bed early, but all was quiet. It wasn't until the next night that news came. Mr. Ralph from Cooper's Community Store brought the telegram to the house, and she knew it held bad news before she opened it. It did, indeed. Their brother Richard had died that afternoon in Conway, quite unexpectedly, the telegram said.

The whole family was heartbroken, and arrangements were made for Minnie, Sarah Jane, and Granny Cribb to get to Conway as soon as possible for Richard's laying out and burial. It was a long and tiring trip, especially for Granny Cribb. After arriving in Conway and reuniting with family, they learned more sad news. Richard's grown son, Cleveland, had recently been diagnosed with leukemia.

When they returned home some days later, Granny Cribb was exhausted and took to her bed. Her family assumed it was the grief of burying her oldest son and the sad news of her grandson's illness. They hoped time would lessen the grief and she would become functional again. Her grandchildren took turns sitting in the rocking chair by her bed and begged her to tell the old stories she loved to tell, but all she would do was sleep.

Within a few months, Minnie received another telegram from Conway, saying Cleveland was much worse, and if the family in Columbia wanted to see him again, they had better come soon. It was decided Minnie and Sarah Jane would go. On the Wednesday morning they were to leave, their mother summoned them to her bedside with a specific message for Cleveland: "Tell Cleveland I'll see him early Sunday morning."

Assuming she was overcome with emotion, they tried to soothe her. She looked at them with more clarity than she'd shown in months and again said, "Tell Cleveland I'll see him early Sunday morning." They both kissed her and promised to deliver the strange message. When they arrived in Conway, they weren't able to keep their promise; Cleveland was in a coma and never regained consciousness. He died on Friday, and their mother died two days later, early Sunday morning.

My family's not superstitious. Not really. We just believe there are some things that can't be explained, and it's best not to try.

Bradford House

Laura Haddock

To hear the old aunties tell it, Bradford House has more ghosts than a hound has itches. Of course, they are only the best type of ghosts—genteel ladies in hoop skirts and compliant servants in headscarves. At least those are the ones they'll discuss in front of company.

I grew up in the house, so I know the rest.

"It's good for business, at least," Aunt Hattie told me. She had me show her how to post comments on TripAdvisor and set up a website for the inn. Once she figured out the potential, she coordinated an October ghost week with the Memphis travel bureau that started with a walking tour through Elmwood and ended with dinner and an overnight stay at the Bradford at a *ghostly good rate*!

Every little bit helped, what with the recession and the raise on minimum wage. We were down to one nonfamily employee, Titia. She was lazy and often late, but nobody could match her biscuits. Bradford Biscuits. We were famous for them.

The aunties converted the family house to an inn nine years ago, when the last of the Bradford men passed this life. Monroe T. Bradford, my uncle, went *before his time*, according to Aunt Lenore. It couldn't have come sooner, if you asked most folks. Monroe may have been a business success, but he was a drunk and a letch, and the ghosts all despised him. The official cause of death was accidental—broken neck—but I know the house did him in. *Which* one of them pushed him, I don't know, but young as I was at the time, I still sensed the absolute glee with which all our specters flew about the house, singing,

"Deaddeaddeaddeaddeaddead!"

Everybody hated Uncle Monroe, which is why I couldn't understand when Aunt Lenore decided to bring him back. She hemmed and hawed and danced around the subject until, finally, Aunt Hattie caught on.

"Jesus H., Lenore, please tell me you do *not* intend to call back Monroe. I will not have that man back in my house, dead or no."

"Hattie, it's only that I need to ask him about the key. It's driving me to distraction not knowing what it fits." Lenore's hands trembled as she poured the sweet tea. "Couldn't we just bring him back *temporary*-like?"

In the end, Hattie threw up her hands and agreed to let Lenore ask Titia to do a calling spell for Monroe, but only if they finished and sent him packing before the guests arrived next week for the Victoriana Fair.

Titia sent me out to pick the herbs from the kitchen garden. "Rosemary, thyme, and the one with the red flower," she instructed. "And the one that smells like pineapple." She pulled down jars full of ugly dried things that may have once been animals and commenced to mixing it all up in her special pot. "Get the aunties," she said.

By now, the ghosties were aware that something was brewing, and they filled the corners of the kitchen and sat in every chair so that *we* all had to stand. I could sense their excitement.

Titia hummed as she stirred, and the room grew hot, and I felt drowsy. I found a vacant spot under the table and lay down for a minute to cool off. The next thing I knew, Hattie was shaking me. "Get up, Annalee. We've got a mess on our hands. Get on up now."

The kitchen was full of smoke, and Hattie was waving a *Ladies' Home Journal* around to clear the air. "What happened?" I asked, but right away, I knew. When the ghosties realized who Titia was calling from the other side, they ruined the spell.

"It just went wrong is all," said Aunt Hattie. "Shouldn't be knocking on that door anyway, if you ask me. It's unnatural." Titia rolled her eyes at this and set her pot to soak.

Aunt Lenore paced the kitchen, wringing her hands, and I felt sore sorry for her until I had a thought.

"Aunt Lennie," I said. "What if we don't even need old Uncle Monroe?"

"What do you mean, child?"

"I just wonder if maybe one of the others knows about the key?" As soon as I said it, I felt a cold pinch on my shoulder. It was the young lady from the attic. We weren't the best of friends, but she wasn't the devious sort, so I knew she meant to help. I held out my hand, and Aunt Lenore passed me the key, which immediately flew up and out of the room.

"Run!" I yelled and chased after, with Aunt Hattie, Lenore, and Titia following. I thought I'd lost it, but there on the stairs, the key hovered in midair waiting for us. We followed along, up two flights to the attic. We lost Titia halfway, when she sat down to catch her breath, but the aunties and I gathered around and waited to see what happened next.

"What now?" Hattie asked.

I was about to answer with something smart-mouthed when the attic door slammed, and we all jumped. Aunt Lenore covered her face, and I thought she might faint.

"Well, that was a nasty trick," Hattie said. I agreed, but it didn't seem like something the young woman of the attic would do. Then I saw—

"Would you look at that?" Behind the door was a wall safe, hidden until now.

"Well, I'll be," Hattie said.

"Oh, bless your heart!" Lenore said to the ghost.

"What do you suppose Monroe kept in there?"

"Let's find out," I said. I tried the key, and after a couple of jiggles, the lock caught and the safe opened. Lenore dove right in, rifling through the stacks of money. "What are you looking for, Aunt Lennie?"

"Oh, I don't know. I thought there might be a note or something. Nothing but money." She looked disappointed. "I just thought maybe Monroe left me something special."

"I'm sorry, Auntie," I said. "At least now we don't have to rent out rooms." Now I noticed that Aunt Hattie looked downcast.

"I don't see why we can't keep the inn open. I like it myself. Keeps a soul busy."

So we decided to use some of Uncle Monroe's money to paint and spruce up, and the house seemed happy with this. There was enough left for me to start college next year and for Hattie to design and print a new brochure for Bradford House Inn, Home of the Bradford Biscuit. She left off the ghosties this time to try a new slant.

Lenore splurged and took the Amtrak to New Orleans with her church group, and when she came home, she seemed all aglow. Aunt Hattie thinks she met someone.

I just hope the ghosts like him.

Storm Fronts
Michael Hodges

The doe bounded through the woods of North Carolina, leaping over deadfalls and brambles. Behind her, the dark sky rumbled, the clouds a dense mixture of white, black, and steel. The rain plunged into the canopy in sheets and fell to the ground through layers of vegetation. Sweet grass and ferns received the cool water with verdant arms.

The doe moved to a patch of spruce, using it as a shield from the cold rain. She twitched her tail and dug a hoof into the soft soil, her breath hushed by the pattering drops.

Perfect, Jansen thought. He sat twenty feet high in his deer stand, wearing a camouflage weatherproof poncho and an orange wool cap. He adjusted his shooting glasses with his left hand and then pulled the trigger. The Winchester rifle flashed and crackled through the woods. The doe took a half-breath and slumped to the forest floor, held by a brace of lady fern and dead aspen branches. Blood trickled from her tan hide onto a carpet of spruce needles. Still now. Brown eyes open and lifeless.

Jansen slung the rifle around his shoulder and climbed down. *Careful, you don't want an injury all the way out here*, he thought. Jansen trotted to the deer, pulse racing.

"Gotcha," he said to the forest, patting the deer on the side. "You'll feed me for a long time."

He looked to the canopy, noticing the rain had stopped. He removed a massive knife from his hip belt, the blade at least ten inches long. Jansen field-dressed the animal, cutting along the center of the stomach north then south. The knife ripped through tough skin and sinew, and the guts of the thing slithered out like bloody balloon animals. The forest taking back what it gave. He cut with zeal, eyes dancing as the stench of fresh organs permeated the area. Satisfied, Jansen began pulling the animal to his ATV just over the rise. He grunted as he dragged the deer, jerking it hard when it caught on a branch. A trail of slime flowed out behind him, mixing with the pungent needles and vibrant leaves. When Jansen reached the ATV, he laid the deer into a metal trailer and surveyed the forest. *Twenty more days of hunting season*, he thought, *and ten more tags to fill.* The Department of Natural Resources awarded him a surplus this year, thanks to a rising population. Some of the men back in town said that a high density of logging roads combined with climate change had allowed for white-tailed deer to explode in numbers. He didn't know about all that, but he knew there was a hell of a lot of deer. Jansen started the ATV and followed his own personally cut trail back to the cabin, the trees flushing cool drops of water onto his poncho. Hemlock, aspen, white pine, and red pine guarded his path home, and creatures in all directions scurried away from the sound of the motor. Agile wings flashed behind countless trunks, and the rumps of black bears disappeared into bogs.

The cabin was made of dark logs, and in the center, a stone fireplace rose to a vaulted ceiling. He'd built it for Dolores, who was long gone, God bless her. She'd died from lung cancer a year ago, her oxygen mask still sitting on her oak dresser in their bedroom. It'd been a hard year, the hardest he'd ever known. She'd been his only true friend. All he had left now was the woods—not the best companion for conversation, although he tried.

Jansen entered the cabin, sat on a Santa Fe–patterned couch, and put a bottle of Seagram's to his lips. *I earned all of this*, he thought. A sigh of pleasure escaped his throat, and he belched and walked back outside. He unhinged the metal trailer and rolled it into the garage. Inside were worktables pushed against the walls, and on the ceiling hung three sturdy hooks. Jansen took a white stepladder, slid it under a random hook, and set the deer by the hole in its chest. It hung there, neck bent, tongue lolling. Jansen stepped back and observed the deer with a grin. *Nice start to the season*, he thought. His hungry eyes scanned the animal, and he noticed a white pattern on the deer's right side, like a brand. Two white lines, each six inches long, crossed each other at the center. He raised an eyebrow and thought of a game farm.

"Nah," he said to the dead deer. "You aren't from a game farm." He knew the closest game farm was at least a hundred miles away. Sure, a deer could cover the distance, but the odds were low. *Just a peculiar marking is all—like a birthmark.* Jansen quartered the deer, placing the chunks into neat rows inside the horizontal garage freezer. He needed to make room for much more.

The morning air tingled with the promise of fresh venison. He rode his ATV to the deer stand predawn, the engine puttering, one headlight searching in the silhouettes of trees. Bats ravaged insects above the canopy, and a flying squirrel made its last stunt before light, chortling as it glided. Billowing mist swallowed the forest, masking the trunks of older trees and obscuring the young spruce. Jansen listened to the woods, the pileated woodpecker hammering for grubs, the ruffed grouse thumping its wings. To the west, a portentous black sky. Lightning flashed sideways from a monstrous thunderhead. Seventy yards behind him, chunks of hail rattled against branches and leaves, inching closer. The Birth-Mother. Sustenance. Falling thousands of times before and a thousand times to come, falling on the stone houses of generations and the old-growth forest that man would not or could not cut. For as long as rain falls, man will walk the earth or nurture the soil with his bones. And those bones will rise up from the rain, the Birth-Mother. The Dream-Maker. All that is possible and all that will ever be, shifting shadows deep in moist glades bespeckled with fireflies. Wood anemones and lady fern framing an aqua creek pool, the black rock slick. All that is possible. All that came to be. There, there, in the woods.

Jansen heard the running deer.

It came from the direction of the storm, panting and leaping. Another doe. She stopped, glanced back to the storm, puttered forward, and settled behind a maple tree.

Jansen aimed the rifle and squeezed the trigger. The deer bolted, running forty yards and then collapsing into a pile of yellow and crimson leaves. Jansen climbed down from the stand. His bad knee twitched as he ran, sending shards of discomfort through his upper leg. The hail pelted his rain gear and stung the exposed skin on his wrists. Jansen reached the deer, aimed his rifle at her head, and fired. The doe fell still. He stood and stared, his chest heaving. The hail salted both of them, the soft patter of tiny water cubes on the taut deer carcass and soaked leaves. As he went to gut the deer, the hail stopped. A cold wind sighed through the forest, scattering vibrant leaves in unpredictable patterns. A whiff of ozone washed across his face. Lightning flashed, and Jansen felt a tinge of nausea, followed by guilt. He'd never felt guilty, not even when he ran out of the mine shaft, leaving four men behind. If he hadn't, he would've been yellow bones in a cave too. Jansen wiped the rain from his face and gutted the animal, his enthusiasm waning.

Jansen transported the deer home and hung it on one of the garage hooks. He was admiring the animal when he noticed another white mark on the right side—two white lines crossed at the center.

"What the hell is going on?" he said to the hanging deer. "I think I shot you yesterday."

Jansen ran two fingers along the mark, pushing back the coarse hairs. He quartered the deer and placed the chunks inside the freezer. He stepped back and shut the lid as his mind offered an incomplete thought. Something inside him twitched as if his world was out of alignment. *You're going senile,* he thought.

Jansen drove to the stand in early morning darkness, the sky packed with stars, sometimes eclipsed by curtains of trees and their veinlike branches. He climbed using the faded wooden steps he'd hammered into the maple years ago and sat on the narrow platform. The clean crisp air combined with the scent of wet leaves pleased his senses. A whippoorwill echoed across the forest. It was in these moments he thought of Dolores and her comforting eyes and warm embrace. Jansen did not care to think of how she died, but in a way, it made him not think about the other *thing* as much.

He studied the forest he'd known all his life. He'd worked for forty years just twenty miles from here over at Harper's mine in Weaverville. He was no longer a miner. Some didn't get a choice like he did, certainly not the four men in shaft 17. His mind went down to that disconsolate place, the dead white branches with elastic bands and bulbs on stonelike skulls. He tried to imagine what their screams sounded like, absorbed by tons of earth. He had missed that fate by only a few feet. *No use to dwell on it*, he thought. *No damn use at all.*

Jansen took a Thermos from his backpack and poured the steaming coffee into a plastic cup. The coffee warmed his hands as he sipped. His eyelids drooped, the caffeine not having the desired effect. He dozed off, holding the cup in his lap with both hands.

Thunder shook the woods, stirring Jansen from his sleep. The light was grey, the air cooler. He rubbed the cobwebs from his eyes and looked for signs of deer. The sky roared once more. *Another morning, another storm*, he thought. A frantic wind bullied the trees, and the ferns sang with its enthusiasm. Then Jansen heard panting. Running from the storm was another doe. She bounded north, south, and then east, confused. She stopped twenty yards from his position, and he fired, the rifle crackling through the woods, followed by a long low rumble. Lightning flashed to the eastern horizon, and gobs of rain fell, setting off whispers and promises of life. The doe fell, mouth open, tongue out. The rain dripped onto her soft eye, trickling down the curve of it. Jansen reached the animal and observed the hide. She was lying on her right side, so he flipped her over. His eyes went wide and his throat grew dry when he saw the mark. His lips moved, but he never heard himself say anything.

"Well, I'll be," he said. His mind went to the freezer and how he would feed himself over the winter. The union had reduced his pension, and his food budget was problematic. *An old man's got to eat*, he thought. He'd worked his tail off for decades. He'd earned a retirement, earned this venison.

At the cabin, Jansen quartered the deer and placed the meat in the freezer. He went to bed, his head swirling with whiskey and the ambiance of the drenched landscape. The image of the soft deer eye, thick lashes, and chromatic leaves filled the back of his eyelids.

The night saw him through, although what happened out there in its completion beyond his log walls, he could not entirely know. But he knew of the calming tones of the great horned owl and the curious, scratching paws of hungry raccoons against the logs. He knew of the strange gawking and squawking night birds. All comforting sounds ushering sleep, sleep. Spiderwebs catching diamonds in the moonlight. A spastic ruffling of feathers and breast under a furry paw and ghostlike eyes. Small claws scurrying up branches. The wind, sent from several fronts by a vengeful general, his eyes mad red. Above the canopy, constellations which glimmer in their triumph over men. The woods were all of that separate, and all of that at once. And then separate again. The wholeness was overwhelming, and when he thought his mind and heart couldn't take it anymore, he drifted off.

He drove to the deer stand at sunrise, catching a glimpse of a coyote before it disappeared into a grove of aspen.

As he climbed the deer stand, thunder shook the tree. Jansen hadn't heard it this bad since his trip to Yellowstone. The sky ruptured, sending lightning down to hapless trees miles to the west. Rain pelted the droopy, inundated leaves. Jansen put on his poncho and groaned. A twig snapped, followed by rumbling and a gust of crisp air. A doe bounded into view, her mouth open as she sucked air. She stopped, raised her hooves, and lowered them in place, kicking up soaked pine needles and sand. She stared east, twitched her ears, ran in that direction, and halted once more. Jansen gazed at the doe, waiting for her to show her right flank. She did, and he saw the mark, same as the others. He didn't want to fire, but his hunger screamed at him to pull the trigger.

The doe ran ten yards and collapsed. As he field-dressed the animal, the rain stopped, replaced by his tears. *What the hell is wrong with me?* he wondered.

He sat on the couch, whiskey coating the pin pricks of darkness, which beguiled him these last few days. The big triangle windows in the north wall let in dusk, as if he had to put them there for fear of dusk's Revealer issuing a decree at his disobedience, as if his log cabin was an unwelcome blemish in what the Revealer had designs for. The big triangle windows were always meant to be at that spot, in this time, just for that specific ray of light. Jansen leaned back and stretched. He would survive the winter without asking for handouts after all.

"Thank you, Mother Nature," he said to the room. He raised his glass, chinking the ice, and then sipped the brusque whiskey. Jansen crafted a fine evening meal of venison, asparagus, baked potato, and whiskey on the rocks. He put on his favorite Johnny Cash album, *At Folsom Prison*. Jansen tapped his fork on the table, playing the drum part. He hummed the melody to "Dark as the Dungeon," the ambiance of the wild and the alcohol a pleasant mix.

The phone rang at 9:00 pm, jarring him from his meditative state. He wondered who could be calling him. He only had a few acquaintances left.

"Yeah, Jansen here."

"Hey, it's Wilkins. You got a minute?"

"You're interrupting my whiskey hour," Jansen said, happy to hear another voice. "Of course I've got a minute. You do know who you're talking to, right?" Jansen was happy to hear another voice.

There was silence, and Jansen's smile softened.

"They finally opened it," Wilkins said.

Jansen's smile bowed into a grimace as his mind reached out into the darkness, picturing the men and the fear.

"They didn't find 'em," Wilkins said.

Jansen's stomach churned.

"Didn't find them? They were there. I saw them before the earth came down! How could they not be there?"

"I dunno, but they weren't."

"Wrong shaft. They screwed up somehow," Jansen said, trembling.

"No, they didn't, buddy. They got the right one, trust me. I spoke with Harper himself and one of his engineers."

"Bullshit. They had to be there."

"Well, they did find something." Wilkins paused, letting silence grow between them. "On the rocks were four marks. This sounds weird, but they were just two crossed white lines, about six inches or so. The reentry team thought they might have been carved by the men, but no such luck. It wasn't fingernails or chalk." Wilkins paused again. "That's all I got, pal. Sorry to bother you, but I figured you should be the first to know."

Jansen dropped the phone, and it pulled the receiver onto the floor. He clutched his thinning hair as his eyes darted around the cabin. Then he ran to the garage and flung open the freezer, gazing into it, the air frosting the tip of his nose. *It couldn't be*, he thought. *It just couldn't be, not in a million years.* He hurried to the work bench and flipped over one of the drying hides. He ran his fingers through the mark, mewling. Jansen opened the garage door and looked into the woods, breathing deeply, the fresh air calming him. A chorus of frogs sang from some unseen pool. The childlike cry of a bobcat came from the east, up near one of the higher pieces of land. Dusk was evaporating into night, the forest never dormant.

The Healer

Josh Strnad

"It's a miracle!"

The crowd cheered, and the organ surged, drowning out the noisy creaking of the frogs and crickets outside. Although it was one of the hottest nights they'd had all summer, the entire town, or all of it that counted, had packed itself into the humble one-room church. It was more crowded that Thursday night than it was on Sunday mornings.

Ahab Shore ran across the front of the sanctuary, bending and twisting his spine in every direction. He threw his cane away in his joy, and it clattered to the floor. The fact that it didn't hit anybody was a small miracle in itself, considering how dense the crowd was.

"I'm healed!" he shouted, jumping up and clicking his heels. His snaggletoothed grin shone from the midst of his greying beard. "The pain is gone! My back is completely healed!" Ahab began to dance a jig, gripping his belt with both hands and stomping his boots on the rough wooden floor. The crowd joined in the pandemonium, hooting and hollering and clapping their hands. Jeremiah Colton was the only one not jumping about. He remained seated in his chair in the middle of the stage, a placid smile on his face.

"Heal me too!" Delilah O'Connor shouted from the crowd. People moved aside to let the heavyset woman pass. "For the love of God, heal me too!" She coughed violently into her handkerchief, leaving a bright red stain. As quick as they had begun celebrating, the people quieted down, turning their eyes to Jeremiah.

The young man said nothing, but that didn't surprise anybody. No one in the town had ever heard Jeremiah speak. They had thought him a bit touched. Maybe he was, for all they knew. It didn't make no difference. He had a gift.

Jeremiah nodded and gestured for Delilah to come forward. Hacking and retching, she sidled out of the pew and waddled toward the stage. Jeremiah watched her come, his quiet steady gaze never leaving her pained features. When she had climbed the steps and reached the chair, she knelt with some difficulty so that she was at eye level with Jeremiah.

A hush fell over the congregation as Jeremiah Colton reached out toward Delilah. She shook with another coughing fit, but he managed to catch her shoulders, holding his hands there with purposeful intensity. He shut his eyes, and his face took on a strained expression.

It was over in a moment. That was all it took.

Delilah jumped up, radiant with joy and practically glowing with health. She drew a deep breath and released it slowly, savoring the air. Everyone could tell she was not the sickly woman she had been just seconds before. She threw back her head and laughed. Many laughed with her. Organ music swelled through the sanctuary. Shouts of joy rose from every corner of the room.

"She's healed!"

"Praise God!"

"Praise *Jesus*!"

Chaos ruled for the next few minutes. The windowpanes rattled with the noise. The room sweltered like an oven.

In the midst of the celebration, the people almost didn't notice Cain Riggins, leading his ten-year-old daughter Martha by the hand through the throng. They were almost to the stage before people saw them at all. When they did, an immediate hush fell over the crowd; the noise died so suddenly that it was like flicking off a radio. Slowly, carefully, Cain led his blind daughter to the foot of Jeremiah's chair.

When they stopped, Martha reached out to touch Jeremiah's face, reading his features with her soft small hands. He let her. The only noises were the insects and frogs singing outside and the flutter of people fanning themselves with pieces of paper.

Jeremiah looked up at Cain, who nudged his little girl in the back. "Please," she said, her small voice full of hope, "I'd like to be able to see. Can you do that? For me?"

Jeremiah nodded, shut his eyes, and placed his hands on Martha's shoulders. The expression of strain flitted across his features and was gone.

Martha's vacant stare underwent an instant transformation. Her pupils dilated, and she looked first from Jeremiah and then to her father. "Pa!" she shouted, her face a perfect display of wonder and delight. "It's true! I can see!"

Cain, laughing and weeping at the same time, scooped his daughter up and looked deep into her eyes. "She can see!" he shouted. "My little girl is healed!"

The crowd went crazy. The organist didn't even bother to play any music but joined the others in shouting and dancing in the aisles.

"Praise the Lord!"

"Hallelujah!"

Jeremiah just sat in his chair, peaceful and quiet amid the overjoyed townspeople. Cain bent down and grabbed Jeremiah's hand between both of his own. "Thank you," he whispered, all but inaudible beneath the shouting congregation. "Thank you."

Jeremiah said nothing. He smiled and inclined his head in acknowledgment.

The celebration in the little church lasted for hours. It was late at night when, at last, the party began to wear down. One by one, the people returned home to their beds, where they would dream about the marvelous things they had seen that night.

When everyone else had gone, Jeremiah Colton was left alone, still sitting on the stage—the first to arrive and the last to leave. With a heavy sigh, he rose from his chair, hunching over and putting a hand on his back as white-hot pain shot through it like molten lead. As he started toward the steps, he let out a terrible rattly cough from deep in his lungs. He turned his head aside, choking and unable to breathe, and spat a mouthful of phlegm and blood onto the floor. He had to stand still for a moment, focusing in order to recover his breath. Then careful not to fall, he began feeling his way blindly along, first, the stairs, then the rows of pews, making his way toward the church exit.

A True Story about the Devil and Jamie's Shoes

Megan Engelhardt

One Saturday, my brother Jeff and our pal Jamie and I were coming home from a day's fishing. Our poles made shadows on the road, and the laces on Jamie's shoes were flapping, kicking up little puffs of dust.

Since it was summer, Jamie was the only one wearing shoes. He never went barefoot, even though his mama tried to make him save his shoes for school and church and threatened his life if he ever lost them. We asked what was wrong with squishing through mud and marsh like the rest of us, and he took off the shoes and showed us the paper that lined the insides. Turned out that Jamie was superstitious. Last year at the county fair, an old woman told him to write the names of the apostles on a piece of paper and put it inside his shoes for good luck. Now Jamie is also sloppy and couldn't keep his shoes tied tight. He always had extra scraps of paper ready in his pockets just in case the ones in his shoes fell out.

We came up on the crossroads where Main Street runs out of town and all the way over to Durham, and there was old Peg Barnes, leaning against the telephone pole. His wooden leg tapped against the crutch he used, and his grizzled hair stood out all around his face. As we went past, he grunted, "This is it." We looked around.

"This is what?" I asked.

"This is where I met the devil."

Jamie got a little pale.

"They say never make a crossroads bargain," Peg said. "But I wanted my leg back. So I came down here at midnight and shed my blood, and when he came, I made a deal."

Jamie was listening with wide eyes, and Jeff was too.

"What kind of deal?" I asked.

"Old Scratch needs someone," Peg said, "to stoke the furnaces away down in hell. That's what he wanted—two men to do his bidding. I told him I'd bring him his men, sure, right here to this crossroads. And here we are. I figure a boy's as good as a man to the devil." He looked over at Jeff and winked. My brother started to cry.

"You stop," I told Peg. "It's gone far enough. Say you're joking."

"No joke," Peg said. "I made the deal, and I'd do it again."

The wind kicked up, and the sky got dark. We blinked the dust from our eyes, and when we could see, there was a man.

I tell you, the devil didn't look like much. I've seen finer men, but he wasn't shabby; and I've seen uglier men, but he wasn't handsome. He looked like every other fellow on the street. I could tell he was the devil, though. It was all around him.

"Afternoon," he greeted us. "How was the fishing?"

"Never mind that. I've got what you asked for," Peg said.

"Boys, not men," said Mr. Scratch, studying us.

"They're strong boys, big enough to do a man's work," Peg said. "I don't care which two you take. Just give me my leg back."

The devil looked at us and opened his mouth and said, "I choose—"

"Wait!" Peg said. "Give me my leg first, or else you don't get any."

Scratch gave him a look but waved his hands. Peg dropped his crutch, and the peg fell off as his leg filled out. Peg stared down at his two good legs and then took a few steps and whooped. He ran in a circle, laughing.

"My turn," Scratch said and pointed. "You and you."

First, I thought, *Thank the Lord* because it wasn't me or Jeff. Then I thought, *Poor Jamie,* and then I thought, *Good* because the devil had also chosen Peg.

Peg stopped running the moment the devil's finger tagged him.

"Well, boys," Scratch said, "it's time to go."

He gave a raucous laugh. With a whoosh of dust and the rush of hundreds of wings, he turned into a giant crow that picked up Peg in one claw and Jamie in the other.

Now this is where Jamie's shoes saved the day. As the devil flew into the air, Jamie's shoelaces wrapped around the telephone wire that hung over the crossroads. The laces tangled and caught, and there was Jamie, hanging from the devil's own claws, stuck on the wire.

The devil glared back, but no matter how he flapped and pulled, Jamie wasn't going anywhere. It didn't make sense how he stayed in those floppy shoes. The only thing we could think was that those apostles' names held him fast. He wasn't coming out of those shoes, though, and those shoes weren't coming off that wire. Scratch thought for a moment and then flew under the wire, giving the laces some slack, hoping they'd come unstuck and let him carry away his prey. He shook Jamie a little, and a scrap of paper came floating out of Jamie's pocket. It hit the devil square between his eyes.

Scratch squealed, shaking his head to get it off, but it was stuck fast. Jamie wiggled a bit, and another scrap came down, and then it was snowing paper, a white blizzard of apostles' names swirling out of Jamie's pants.

You know how sometimes you're so scared you come out the other side where it hits you as funny, and you laugh because there's nothing else for it? That's what happened to us when Jamie's scraps kept falling.

So there's the devil, and there's Jamie, stuck, and there were Jeff and me, laughing. The devil hates being laughed at, and those papers must have hurt him something bad. Faced with that, Mr. Scratch must have decided that one man was good enough. He gave up on Jamie and left, Peg still hanging from the other claw. The papers stopped falling as soon as the devil let go, and Jamie dropped, barefoot, to the ground.

No matter how we tried, we never could get those shoes off the wires. Jamie got a hiding when his mama found he'd lost them, though. You can laugh at the devil, but there's not much you can do about mothers when it comes to shoes.

Murdock

Chris Dezarn

The first time wuz an accident. Hell, the whole deal wuz an accident when yuh git right down to it. We weren't lookin' fur this place. No, sir. We's jus' a couple dumb ol' country boys tryin' to dig a well on Scottie's property. Lookin' fur water, yuh see?

Course, water ain't what we found. But I'll git to that in a minute.

Yuh see, when the economy went to shit, Scottie decided to start tryin' to save every nickel he could. And that wuz one a his ideas.

Yeah, that wuz Scottie, all right. He wuz jus' full a ideas. Git-rich-quick stuff, mostly. Course, none a his schemes ever worked out. Figures he'd luck into this here bi'ness like a blind man pickin' his favorite color socks—by mere chance, that is.

It wuz actually Duke, Scottie's ol' bluetick hound, that found the hole. Yuh see, we's drillin' fur an old aquifer Scottie vowed wuz down there in the ground sum'ers. Then we hit sumthin' harder'n Ol' Scratch's heart. We couldn't be sure, but we jus' figured it wuz a boulder or sumthin' stoppin' us.

But anyways.

Scottie's daddy wuz a miner once upon a time, yuh see, and it jus' so happened that he'd left sum a that old dynamite tucked away in a shed when he up and left this world fur the next un. So we decided to blast through. Well, when that boomstick went off, it musta jarred sumthin' loose down there in the earth 'cause right then, this big ol' dust cloud mushroomed up from the ground 'bout sixty feet from where we's standin'. Then the ground kinda gave way underneath that geyser a dirt and rock, sorta like how a cake yuh're bakin'll fall into its pan if yuh bump the oven or stomp the floor at the wrong time. We jus' reckoned we'd shook open a sinkhole or sumthin'.

Well, to be *completely* honest, we didn't know what the hell we'd found. I tell yuh, we's pretty durn speechless there fur a minute or two. So we went over to check out this big crater in the ground that hadn't been there a minute ago, Duke trailing by Scottie's side like he always done. There wuz this real strong smell comin' up outta there—a kinda vinegary smell that put me in the mind a moldy root cellars and what my pappy always said wuz a sure sign a the dirt goin' sour. Prob'ly sum kinda gas, I s'pose. I know, it don't smell now; it's had plenty a time to air out, I reckon.

But anyways.

We's standin' by the rim a this crater, right—me, Scottie, and Duke—when that ol' hound dog starts goin' off! And I mean go-in-*off*! Actin' like he'd done spied a critter and aimed to have it! And all the while lookin' down in this here pit.

Me and Scottie, we didn't know what to make of it. Scottie yelled fur Duke to shut up, but yuh know how dogs is once they git riled up; there ain't no pacifyin' 'em.

So next thang we know, Duke's heading down in that crater, runnin' right down the loose dirt that sloped to the bottom, movin' like his ass wuz on fire and his head wuz a-catchin'. Well, Scottie goes after him, pickin' his path real careful like— he weren't as nimble as Duke, yuh see. And then there I go after Scottie.

Well, we git to the bottom, right, and Duke's already made the distance to the other side a the bowl.

That's when we noticed the cave. Yeah, that one right over there. Don't look like much, does it? Barely big enough fur a man on his hands and knees to wiggle through. But it's plenty big enough fur an ol' bluetick hound that thinks he's on the trail a game. And yuh *know* that's jus' what happened. Duke shot into that hole without even pausing to think it over, all the while Scottie yellin', "Come back here, yuh dumb sum'bitch!"

Well, Duke didn't come back. But he found what he's after. Yes, sir. 'Cause we start hearin' Duke barkin' and growlin', that kinda ruckus yuh only hear dogs make when they finally git a hold a what they're after. And fur the next few minutes, that's all we heard—Duke fightin'. We could hear what he's fightin' too, though I don't rightly know how to describe what *it* sounded like. I guess, maybe if you's one a them genetic fellers and you's to cross a mountain lion and a Chihuahua—and yes, I'm aware a how silly that sounds; don't even go there— well, it might sound sumthin' that.

Anyways, ever'thang went all quiet again after a minute or two.

When Duke didn't come out right away, Scottie started hollerin' fur him. When he *still* didn't come—didn't bark or nuthin'—Scottie wanted to crawl in there and git him. I had to hold Scottie back, make him realize jus' what a dumbshit idea *that* wuz.

That's when we hear sumthin' shufflin' round in the loose rocks near the cave's entrance. But whatever *it* wuz, it stayed in there. It didn't so much as poke a toenail outside those shadows clustered round the mouth a that cave—and after ever'thang I'd jus' heard, I weren't too sure I wanted to see it anyway.

But what happened next really threw us.

All of a sudden, sumthin' come flyin' at us outta the darkness. I 'bout turned tail and runned right then 'cause I didn't know what wuz a-comin' outta that hole. I jus' knew that if Duke couldn't handle it with his teeth and claws, I sure as damn it wasn't gonna hurt it with the handful a nuthin' I had on me.

But it weren't no swarm a angry little critters.

And it weren't dislodged rocks signalin' another collapse in the earth neither, which is what Scottie later admitted he thought it wuz.

It wuz coins. 'Bout a handful of 'em. Wet with Duke's blood. Once we started really lookin' at 'em, we noticed the Confederate States of America stamp on 'em. They's Confederate coins, yuh see, datin' back to the War between the States. Some copper, some silver, pennies, half-dollars—all kinds. Good condition too, considerin' their age and that they'd just been coughed up outta the ground; in fact, the only thang we could tell was wrong with 'em was a little dirt and dog blood.

Where'd they come from? Yeah, that's what we asked ourselves too. We tossed round sum ideas in the days that followed, tryin' to figure out what'd happened. Scottie wuz tore up 'bout Duke, a course, but I think his curiosity—and them coins—helped relieve sum a that grief.

Anyways, after takin' turns shootin' down each other's suggestions, we decided we needed to run an experiment, see if it happened again. So we went to the stockyard and bought a hog—a nice un too—all fattened up and ready fur slaughter. Then we went back to the cave.

Now I don't know if you've ever tried to git a hog into a cave, but let me tell yuh, they don't like it. This one didn't anyway. Maybe he sensed what wuz down there. Or maybe hogs is jus' clausterphobic by nature. I don't know. But it took me and Scottie the better part a an hour to wrestle that bastard into that hole.

And what happened next?

Well, after the squealin' finally stopped, more twinklin' coins come flyin' out. And more of 'em too—'bout two fistfuls a copper, silver, and even a few gold uns mixed in this time, all drippin' with pig blood.

And that pretty much settled it. We's bein' paid. Paid fur . . . well . . . fur bringin' lunch. We figured that whatever's down there don't git out too much and don't have a whole lotta options as to what it gits to eat. Also, it probably ain't got no use fur them coins. Maybe it jus' thinks 'em purty and sees it as fair trade. Maybe it's been jus' familiar enough with man long enough to figure out a little bit a what makes men tick. I don't know. Any exp'anation's as good as the next, I s'pose.

And that's how it started.

Scottie found this guy in the city who dealt with coins and was just as happy as a flea on a dog's ass to buy all we could bring him. Fur a good price too—nuthin' that'd make us millionaires, mind yuh, but enough to keep us both mighty comfy and let us quit our jobs at the factory. Hell, a few a them 1861 Confederate pennies brought 'bout ten thousand each! So three or four times a week, we'd hit the stockyard, buy a pig, calf, or half a dozen chickens, come back, feed our newfound friend, and collect the payment. Me and Scottie had more money than we'd ever had in our lives, and the critter in the cave wuz gittin' fat off all the stuff we's bringin' him.

Oh, there were a few other details to work out, a course. My ol' lady wuz the biggest problem, I guess. She'd git suspicious sumtimes, wonder how I's gittin' all that money—'cause she eventually heard I quit the factory, but I didn't tell her 'bout my new buddy—but she'd let it slide when I'd hand her a few hundreds.

Scottie dubbed the thang in the cave Murdock, after sum creatures in a H. G. Wells story 'bout time travel we'd had to read in high school. I vaguely remembered the story, but Murdock didn't sound quite right to me—close, but not quite right. But I'd read that story when I's jus' a youngun, so I didn't say nuthin'. Besides, the name didn't matter none no ways—we jus' wanted to call it sumthin' besides "that thang in the cave."

And it went pretty smooth like that fur a while.

Then Scottie got greedy.

Yuh see, Scottie wuz always talkin' 'bout Murdock. Wonderin' what he *looked* like. Sayin' he wanted to *see* him.

Me, I didn't care *what* he looked like. Far as I cared, Murdock could look like Miss America or sumthin' right outta one a them zombie movies. I's jus' fine with the way thangs wuz a-goin'. And I told Scottie as much too. I tried to esplain that we's a-makin' out like bandits. As it wuz, only me and him knew 'bout Murdock and that served all parties involved mighty righteously. I said we jus' needed to leave thangs the way they wuz, keep on doin' what we's a-doin', and not take a chance on spoilin' ever'thang.

Well, that seemed to work. Fur a while more, anyways. But like I said, Scottie always had one git-rich-quick scheme or another swimmin' round in that head a his, and he eventually fished up a doozie. He started talkin' 'bout how we'd probably make a fortune if we could sell a picture a Murdock. *A damn picture!*

And the *way* he said it . . .

I think it wuz really more curiosity than greed. Curiosity, and him tryin' to justify it the way men justify jus' 'bout ever'thang—with money.

I tried to make him see how that could backfire, how tellin' people 'bout Murdock might be a bad idea. Told him only a damn fool would trade the cow fur the milk.

I tried . . .

But honestly, I guess I knew he'd already made up his mind. Oh, Scottie . . .

Well, I went over to Scottie's a day or two later to pick him up and head to the market. We'd already decided to start raisin' animals out on Scottie's property, but we weren't to the point where we could forgit 'bout the stockyard jus' yet. His truck wuz in the drive, so I checked inside the house and round, but I didn't find him. I looked fur him fur 'bout fifteen minutes before I remembered his crazy picture idea.

Rememberin' that, I started toward the hole, my guts twistin' into tighter knots with each step fur fear a what I'd find.

And when I got here? Well, I found what I's afraid I would. Sorta, anyway.

Near the entrance, there wuz Scottie's old Polaroid camera, the casing cracked in a couple a places and specked with dried blood.

And there, hangin' out the front—lookin' like sum kinda weird tongue lollin' out an even weirder-lookin' head—there wuz a picture. Now I know yuh want me to tell yuh that that picture finally showed me what wuz in that hole, but it didn't. It wuz jus' shadows fur the most part, although there wuz these white streaks blurred across the middle a the shot—what coulda been a pale hand takin' a swipe at the camera, I guess.

Confederate coins wuz scattered 'bout the ground too. The only difference wuz there wuz more of 'em. A *helluva* lot more. There musta been six or eight handfuls spread over the ground round that camera. And a few looked like they hadn't never even been touched! Yuh shoulda seen the look on our coin guy's face when I brought him *those*!

But yeah. That's what happened to Scottie. I wuz a might troubled 'bout it, a course, but what could I do? Murdock . . . he didn't know no better. He's jus' actin' the way we'd more or less taught him to. It wuz Scottie's fault, really, but yuh can't blame a man fur his curiosity neither, 'cause men are jus' as addicted to their curiosity as junkies are to drugs and politicians are to power.

So that's why I say the first time wuz an accident.

But the *second* time . . .

Well, when my ol' lady started runnin' round with this feller a few towns over . . . yeah, that weren't no accident.

Prosperous, but no accident.

Yuh see, before Scottie . . . yuh know . . . we'd git just a couple handfuls a coins at most. It wuz only after Scottie . . . yuh know . . . that the real payout started. Seems like ol' Murdock'd found sumthin' he really likes, and he don't mind payin' top dollar fur his favorite dish. I can't rightly say as I fully understand his pricin' philos'phy or how or where he got all them coins, but he's a shrewd devil, I tell yuh.

Anyways, that feller my wife wuz a-seein' came nosin' round a few weeks later, lookin' fur the cheatin' bitch.

Eh . . . let's jus' say he found her.

And now here *you* are, lookin' fur Scottie, wantin' him to answer sum damn tax questions and talkin' 'bout takin' his land if he don't. And seein' as how Scottie can't exactly meet with yuh to do that . . .

Well now, I jus' can't have that. I'll have to think up sumthin', I guess, but—

Here now! Quit that! Yuh ain't shuckin' outta that duct tape; I don't care how much yuh squirm. This ain't my first rodeo, so to speak.

Oh, and I'm real sorry yuh gotta be awake fur this—truly, I am—but Murdock . . . well, he likes his meals fresh and wigglin'. I tried a bucket a KFC once, but . . .

Uhmm . . .

Yuh like the bell? It's sumthin' I added to call Murdock when supper's ready. See? It echoes through the cave real nice-like, don't it?

Now don't worry. It'll be quick. It usually is, anyways.

Come on, Murdock! Supper's a-waitin'! I got yuh favorite!

Underwater

Erin Mundy

In 1959, the newly created Lake Lanier reached its normal level of 1,070 feet above sea level for the first time, covering 38,000 acres. The government bought land from over seven hundred families in that area for twenty-five to seventy-five dollars per acre.

The water is cold. Colder than one would expect for the summer, but I am at the bottom of the lake. Down here, the water is black; you and your surface eyes couldn't see your hand until it was almost touching your face. But I can. My eyes never close. I see fish—small, big, frightening. Near me is a tree stump. It's old, ugly, waterlogged, and stiff. Before there was a lake, there was farmland—crops and homes and gardens. They are gone, but there are still trees, stumps, the secret forest that spreads under the waves. Whole trees still stand in some places, their branches just below the surface. Old fishing line is wrapped around it. Fishing line will tangle around you like a python snaring its prey. I feel the muddy sand under me mixed with leaves and roots. Above me are children swimming. They dive from the boat so they can try to touch the bottom. Eyes shut, they hold their breath until they feel the cold sand under their toes. Then they push up as hard as they can so they can once again take a dry gulp of air. They don't see me. Even if their eyes were open, they wouldn't see me. Their eyes are not like my eyes. Above, where the sun touches the water, the parents of the diving children sprawl on their foam floats, letting the lake water cool their hot skin. Boats speed above me, their wake rippling down to me, setting the trees to shudder as though buffeted by a wind. Sometimes the boats pull skiers, wakeboarders, or tubers. Once, I swam, skied, floated, and lived. Now I reside on the lake bottom, where there were crops and homes and gardens. I can no longer remember how I got here. I only know that my fishing line holds me here, among the trees of the eternal forest, long after the lake has washed the other lives away. No one managed to find me. No one ever will.

The End of Grace

Meriah Lysistrata Crawford

On August 23, 2011, at 1:51 pm (EDT), there was an earthquake centered in Louisa County, Virginia, with a magnitude of 5.8. Unlike most earthquakes on the West Coast, where tremors are seldom felt even a state away, this quake was felt for hundreds of miles—as far north as Montreal. According to the United States Geological Survey, this is "due to the ease of wave propagation through the North American craton."

The Virginia quake, as it is now called by people outside of Virginia (we call it the Louisa quake or just the quake), caused extensive damage and shook up millions of people who'd been going about their day believing that the ground was solid beneath their feet. The majority of the damage could be found, not surprisingly, in Louisa County itself. Innumerable chimneys were converted to a scattering of bricks on roofs; two schools were damaged beyond use; a historic nineteenth-century house and church were devastated by the heaving ground. Facades collapsed in front yards. Power lines fell. Dishes and glassware and knickknacks and irreplaceable family heirlooms were smashed on floors for miles around.

In the weeks that followed the quake, FEMA first declined to intervene and then consented. A disaster was declared, inspectors and workers swarmed the county, checks were written, repairs were made—or not, in some cases. The community mourned, came together, and carried on as communities do.

Aftershocks continued for months, leaving everyone on edge, but before long, most people looked back on the quake with a mixture of relief and pride. It was a trial the people had endured, and it would become a story they would tell for the rest of their lives. Not so bad, really, once the fear and frustration and hard work had passed into the dim forgetfulness that time delivers. And anyway, no one had died—that was what really mattered. Or almost no one, anyway.

The Louisa quake was caused by "compressional forces," resulting in "one rocky block being pushed up relative to rock beneath the fault"—so the experts at USGS said with a sort of charming innocence. A geology professor named Callan Bentley, from the University of Virginia in Charlottesville, suggested in a blog post that "differential rebound of the crust due to isostatic adjustments" might be to blame. But an offhand note about his cat near the end of the post brought him closer to the truth: "My cat was hiding in the closet and wouldn't even come out for food." It wasn't just the earthquake that scared Callan's kitty. I'm pretty sure it was me.

I want to state this clear and plain, right off: I didn't know this would happen. I want that clear—not because I think it absolves me of my responsibility, my guilt—but because I would not have ever done it if I'd known what would follow. But how could I? How could I have ever imagined that I might read a few fading lines scribbled on the flyleaf of a battered old cookbook, shed a few drops of blood on the ground, and cause the entire East Coast of the North American continent to pitch and shudder and cry out? It's mad is what it is. I'm mad. Surely.

But I was there, alone in the woods with that cookbook and a sharp paring knife and a world of hate in my heart for that man. That evil man. I sat on a flat rock under a huge pine tree, propped the book open on my knees, and tried, tried, tried to pierce the skin of my palm with that knife. So much harder than I imagined.

I closed my eyes tight and thought of him—his sneering contempt, his refusal to even listen, the way he laughed, finally, when the house collapsed under the assault of the bulldozer. My house. Mother's house. And her father's and his father's, back to 1836. Gone.

And the knife cut in.

Blood pooled in the cup of my hand. I watched it well up and thought of my mother. A strong, vibrant woman a year ago—still tending her small garden. Now unable to cope with the loss of her home . . .

Hatred overflowed with my blood, pattering onto the pine needles and rocks and dirt between my feet. I tipped the book up and read the lines, tilting my hand to speed the flow, filling the words and my blood and the ground beneath my feet with rage. My voice grew louder, and my fury swelled; my fist clenched, and the stream of blood fell faster.

And the earth answered my call. She roared—her cry echoing mine—and then his voice cried out in pain and terror, rising to an impossible crescendo. And finally, the horror of understanding in his screams. Understanding at last.

And then silence.

When the ground had gone still at last, I stumbled back to my car in shock. I drove home, climbed exhausted into bed, and slept. A few hours passed. When I rose, I gaped in horror at the television. *Impossible. Impossible,* I told myself. That could not have been me.

I listened to the men talking on TV about the quake and slowly, inexorably, became convinced they were right. Or almost convinced. Because of the timing—and the fact that it worked. And then I tested it because I had to be sure.

I stepped outside, walked a few minutes into the trees, peeled back a bit of scab—"Ow! Ow! Ow!"—and let a drop of blood hit the dirt. The ground shifted and roared as I fell to the ground, sobbing.

Yes. It was me.

I pressed my shirt firmly to the wound and ran back to the house for a bandage. The USGS reported it as a 4.2 aftershock, occurring at 8:04 pm. One single drop of blood: 4.2. I must not bleed on the ground again. I must not. I called in sick, just to be sure.

And then the next night, in the early hours, I stepped outside to get a better signal on my cell phone, as I had done a million times before, and caught the sole of my foot on a sharp piece of rock. "Ouch!" and "Damn!" and the ground cried out again, as if in sympathy with my pain. I dropped my phone and clutched at the door, dragging myself and my bleeding foot inside as the earth pitched. August 25 at 1:07 am: 4.5.

I called in sick again. And again and again until I was fully healed.

As more time passed and lives returned to normal, I tried to find some peace in my act of vengeance, but there was none. The equation was unequal, and I couldn't fix it. Finally, I understood that the equation had not been mine to work. A line had been crossed that never should have been—and the ground just kept on shaking.

I had to wonder. All this nonsense about seismology and tectonic plates—scientists and studies and charts and monitoring stations and experts expounding unendingly—was any of it real, or was it just a sign of our pathetic need to explain in some vaguely scientific way what can't be explained at all?

In the absence of answers—real answers—I have done what I can. I burned the book. I have left clear instructions that my remains are to be cremated when I die. And I have researched thoroughly and selected what I believe is a safe way to bring my death with all possible haste but without risk of my blood being shed. I can only imagine what the result would be if I were shot or stabbed or hit by a car, causing my blood to drain freely on the ground. I cannot, as the good person I once unhesitatingly knew I was, risk that. Not for anything. For what has already happened, know that I am so, so sorry. If I could undo it, I would. I only hope this works. We will know soon enough.

Florida Natural

Ben Bowlin

https://www.youtube.com/watch?v=DlA7J4rFNTM

It's my turn. The foreman waves his hand, and I'm off, moving before his shoulder twitches, senses magnified, pulse loud and heavy in my ears. Adrenaline burns bright, and I'm dizzy, floating, devoid of body and carton and clothing and mind. Colors sharpen. The stench of ripening oranges pierces my nose, burning the hairs, boring through my sinuses into my brain like those bronze hooks Egyptian embalmers used to harrow through their pharaohs' skulls.

I read the fine print on the cuff of the foreman's tan leather work glove: Rawling and Company. Made in China. I don't slow down to grab a carton anymore. I'm always holding one before it's my turn to run. I can throw a carton with either hand, hitting the hole in the grove precisely, every time. I've never missed. It's at a tricky angle, this hole. You'll hear about other groves with flat spots level to your chest, right in front of you. Who knows what that must be like? It's something I've never experienced. The closest thing I can think of—the sheer, decadent convenience of a hole in a grove that is both chest-level and flat and right in front of you—to tell you the truth, it reminds me of an ATM or those electric fortune-teller booths at carnivals or maybe being born with vestigial wings. But we didn't get to choose where our grove's hole popped up—it was there when we arrived. About eight feet off the ground and at a sloping downward angle, so you could just tip the carton in if you wanted.

Sometimes you hear about guys showing off. Their buddies stand to one side holding a carton. When the foreman swings around, these guys leave empty-handed, and before they reach aisle 15—dairy products, butter, orange juice, and eggs—and before they hit the hole, some joker tosses them a fresh carton, and they pull a move while they catch it, maybe somersaulting or bounding into the air. People applaud. If I have time, I clap too.

We must not resent success.

Sure, we might have our differences, but people are much the same, aren't we? Before my first stint in jail, I had an English professor who always said, "The human race is a team sport." I think about that often. I have this hunch sometimes that we all may as well be the same person. We all want the same Big Things, don't we? Happiness and love and some encounter with infinity? We're headed for the same hopeful places. We differ only in the details. By which I mean I keep my cartons with me. I wait for my turn standing near the pickup full of cartons with one in hand. When the foreman waves, I run. I *haul ass*. I like running, like the way it freshens the air. The orange grove hangs fecund in the harsh sunshine, swaying along the warm unending coastal breeze. I look stupid when I run, I admit. But surrounded by coworkers, appearances become irrelevant, and only our technique matters. Here's mine: a measured sprint to the hole, a running hop, and just as my hand enters the limbo up to the forearm, a small smooth throw-toss of the carton, en-suring we will never touch. It takes seconds. Sometimes I jump too soon, and I have to throw the box from a distance. I'm over-enthusiastic, ungraceful, and effective. I'm the Joe Montana of gently tossed orange juice. My work doesn't look pretty, but again, I have never missed. No Average-Yet-Discriminating Grocery Shopper leaves the orange juice section disappointed, at least not if I have anything to do with it. Running with this fresh carton of orange juice, watching falcons fly in widening orbits above me, I think again of how much I love this. The sheer pursuit of it all. Each time someone at 100 Fairview Road in Ellenwood, Georgia, stops at aisle 15—dairy products, but-ter, orange juice, and eggs—lingering and pushing slowly past the yogurt, we are standing at the ready; the foreman reaches out just as you, Average-Yet-Discriminating Grocery Shopper, reach into the depths of the premium orange juice selection searching for that perfect, obscenely fresh carton—that same burning orange turning my nose inside out as I run—and the foreman holds his hand aloft, and my God, I run past time—I mean, I must because here I am, here it seems I have always been—wrist at the edge of the hole between your grocery store and this grove, my hand stretching into limbo at the same mo-ment yours reaches in, feeling the warm Florida breeze and the reassuring heft of Florida's Own. It reminds me of that Michelangelo painting, the one with the horrible name. God's up there, leaning forward to not-quite-touch Adam Kadmon, who slouches lazily, limp-wristed, hand and finger apathetic. He seems bored of creation even as it occurs. I think about us—you and me, I mean. If we were Adam and God, who would I be? Do our hands radiate heat toward one another? How close are our fingers? If I shed my gloves, would I feel your fingertips brush against my own? I say it again: I suspect we are the same, if only for one unending moment.

Do not fear me; I am a stranger, I am a phantom. My hands are clean, and anyway, whether or not you like it, I am there, and then I am gone. I fall in a neat roll along the ground, panting. I rest ten minutes and head back to my place in line. And you disappear onto a life, one carton of orange juice richer. We are worlds apart, but *vete en paz*, I say.

Go in peace, I beg you. Let these falcons enjoy the show.

But who am I to criticize? I am no one special. I am a two-bit ex-con peddling orange juice, and yes, sometimes I do dream of our hands outstretched in limbo, the hairs on our knuckles brushing. This haunts me. But say, we touch—what then? Between the grove and my hand to the box of orange juice and your cart, a chasm yawns wide and dark and enormous. And in this unknowable space between us lies history. The ghosts of orange juice past, politicians and CEOs parsing graphs, people opening restaurants and refrigerators across the globe on Saturday mornings, shaking sleep from their heads and reaching for something. Whatever this thing they reach for might be—whether or not it actually is orange juice—the desire for success is instinctual, and orange juice is a decent substitute for most of what haunts us. Whatever it is, whatever this *thing* might be, whether we are brushing hands in limbo or fucking or holding each other at a funeral or laughing at a stranger's jokes in bars, that gulf still spreads between us, and I think you will agree it is a distance all its own.

These are the things I dwell on, Average-Yet-Discriminating Grocery Shopper, as I queue up to bring you more orange juice.

I'm riding in the back of a red Ford work truck, passing lines of orange trees. This time of the year, the fruits swell, growing to the size of Christmas ornaments, their golden hues sharpening, fluorescing in the sunshine. If you stand here alone in silence at night, you will actually hear the grove ripen. It groans, slowly, like a building on the verge of collapse. Once the truck hits the main path, the driver accelerates, and we rush along the smooth dirt trail wide enough for three cars, racing falcons beneath the sun. The shadows of these birds outpace us, patches of shade flying above like the shadows of sharks in distant oceans. We're too far away to hear them wailing, but they can surely see our truck from the distance, blooming dirt and mud in a cloud behind us. Old men and children picking oranges glance over their shoulders, anxious to walk home, to eat, to make obeisance, and to sleep. We turn from the path, and I swear the birds change direction to follow us.

I wonder if we're rousing the mice. Or is there something else behind us? Something ahead?

It's Thursday, the last shift of the week. I am not a creative man. You could say my dreams of higher arts died in prison. I still read books sometimes, like you. I do all the other things a normal person would do. Two hours later, I'm leaning against the counter at Poco's, avoiding the gaze of a lonely woman near the corner. We make eye contact, and the night fades into a warm buzzing haze.

Three hours later, I vomit when a fist slams into my stomach, contorting the organs beneath. The lonely woman runs forward, yelling about the police. Someone backhands her, the flat sound of the slap echoing across the room as she falls. My head spins on its own accord, and I cannot turn to see what happens next. The bag falls over my head, threads cinching tight along the seam of my Saint Simon hoodie. I kick a leg behind the strangler's calf and jump back, my hands struggling at the cords. We crash onto the floor, and I headbutt his skull until his grip falls slack. I'm slipping the bag but too slowly entangling my fingers. I wrench it away and face the barrel of a gun, close enough to smell the warm burn of ignited powder, to see the thumb pressing on the trigger. Time slows, and I'm lingering on just the barrel of the gun, the top whorl of the fingerprint on the thumb, the part visible over the trigger until the gunman presses down. The click echoes through the barroom as the jukebox plays merrily on. You know how those moments feel in the movies—the big showdown, the fight scene, and so on? At some point, you have seen these things. We both have—who hasn't? You must have sat in your home so many times, perhaps with a glass of orange juice, watching a showdown or a fight scene and saying to yourself, "How unrealistic. What an unrealistic break in the movie."

This moment is exactly like that, like all those bad movies I know you hate. I'm staring at this gun, and I'm thinking of you saying, "How unrealistic," and I agree. This is *unreal*.

The man holding the gun comes into focus; he wears a pin on his shirt. A Mexican. Worse. A Californian. I have just enough time to notice that I don't hear a gunshot when the butt of the pistol hits square above my left eye, and all the world falls dark, even darker than the bar.

Let me explain the Californians. You'd think we'd be friends, right? Of course. Most people, when they imagine other industries, picture laborers as colleagues. I have done the same. I picture autoworkers banding together and doctors, cops, criminals, and even politicians or professors. But in the orange business, things are different. I have killed many Californians. Given the chance, I hope to do it again. I like to spit on Californians before I kill them, not after. I like them to know it's happening, and I like to watch their faces as they go.

Perhaps this is not a higher art so much as a recurring dream.

All to say that when I do wake up, I am hungover and alarmed to be alive. When I stir in the back of the van, one of the Californians—look at that, an honest-to-God Indian—holds a finger to his lips. The bag is gone. I'm lying across the floor. I smell the carpet, the scent of rancid oranges and speed and laugh. The Indian kicks me toward the wall, along the baseboard, and I've cracked a rib but feel tremendous. No plastic on the carpet means they will not kill me now. I say as much to the Indian, and he looks down at me with an absent smile, like I'm some yearling doe wandering out of the woods. After a long moment, he nods. The other Californians sit along the edges of the van's shadows, unmoving beneath the dislodged swinging light. We drive a long way. They do not let me out of the van, and I don't want to leave. When the van stops for good, I think, I will die. Or at least they will try to kill me. These Californians are lazy and maybe inexperienced.

Who else would duct tape my hands in the front? Don't they know who I am?

They pull me out of the side door, blindfold me, and push me to my knees in the hot dust.

"*¿Es esta el?*" says an unfamiliar old man's voice.

"*Claro que sí,*" says another.

They throw me back into the van and argue. I loosen the blindfold and tear at the duct tape with my teeth, pulling off strips of flesh along with sticky ragged tape fibers. A gunshot shatters the air. I fall to the floor and wriggle to the space between the front seats, praying the gunfire doesn't hit the engine or the gas tank.

Gunfights rarely follow movie scripts; they happen so quickly—in a film, even the minor characters move past crippling injuries for as long as the story or the contract requires. But in real life, everyone, and I do mean everyone, is continually startled by the genuine pain of a gunshot, and a great many bullet wounds are fatal within moments. The side window shatters, and I curl in a tight ball beneath the cascading shards of glass, uncertain if the van is running or if I'm in shock. Something sharp and hot explodes like sunshine through my shoe, through the flesh and bones beneath. I pull my left foot closer as the last two surviving men shout until gunshots interrupt their conversation. Pulling onto the driver's seat, I peer over the window's rim—all dead.

Mostly dead. The van is running, but I have to lean down into the floorboard and pop the emergency brake. More gunshots. I follow the trail in the van, driving carefully until I near the dirt road and see another car wheeling out from behind the shack, giving chase.

Sometimes I wonder if you have been in a car chase. When I'm holding a carton, just before the foreman's hand comes up, I wonder, *Who is this carton for? What type of person wants this orange juice? Surely, orange juice alone does not define an individual. Has this person been in a car chase? Is this person an adventurer, a criminal? Does she or he enjoy pulp?* My heart breaks for you, Average-Yet-Discriminating Grocery Shopper, and I mean this sincerely. You seem so urgent in your need for orange juice. I too feel that certain things cannot wait, and despite the bullet in my left foot and the ding of the low gaslight on the van's dashboard, it occurs to me—again, again, and again—we are very much alike.

The first building I see is a dusty Texaco. The other car still follows behind me. Dark veins of engine smoke bloom in the reflected distance of the rearview, billowing toward the clouds. I pull into the gas station, delirious, thinking of you, thinking of oranges, thinking maybe there's a hole somewhere in here maybe big enough to jump through.

"Holy shit," says the kid behind the counter as I limp toward the drinks along the wall. I wrench open the cooler door and fall against it, my hands bloody and flailing, knocking over bottled water and fruit juice. I hear my own voice yelling in English, in Spanish. I hear the click of the security locks on the door. The kid must have hit the button under the counter, the one clerks use to lock the doors during a robbery. This won't stop the Californians, but it might slow them down. I try to tell this kid not to call the police, tell him that the Californians are above the law and none of us are safe here. There is no hole here in this Texaco juice cooler, only rows of Minute Maid. I collapse. I see the kid running toward me. In one hand, he brandishes a gun and, in another, a first-aid kit. When he sees my ruined foot, he squats down beside me, laying the gun on the floor, and opens the case. He's tying a tourniquet over my left ankle. I tell him not to. I try to tell him we need to leave and leave now.

"Don't worry, I have first-aid training," he says, then something about me being okay and him being a volunteer EMT.

"I'm the Joe Montana of gently tossed orange juice," I say, surprised by the calmness in my voice. I hear sirens in the distance. I tell this kid we are doomed.

The holes have always been here, as far as I know. Our company has never figured out what they come from or what they mean to the world. Scientists have studied the groves. There are conspiracy theories on the Internet, angry politicians, concerned experts. I think it's all bullshit. If the groves were powerful, wouldn't powerful people work there? Wouldn't they have Harvard graduates and decaying aristocrats idling around with prostitutes and cocaine and senators? If the groves are so great, then why are people like me there? We're all ex-cons and immigrants; I've killed eight people, and it wasn't until I accidentally beat a Californian in a bar fight that no other place would hire me. I had no choice other than Florida's Own. This makes no difference to the Californians. Orange juice runs the world, and the masters of California's oranges are no different from my own. A silent war rages for your favor every time you stroll past the dairy aisles, and while most of the casualties are abstract to you, they are very real to me. I am well on my way to becoming one. I must pretend to believe in God, I decide, and pray.

But knowing my luck, God is a Californian.

The police do show, after all, and there's no sign of the car that pursued me through the desert. I'm in a hospital bed, my foot propped up and bandaged. I've been dreaming about those falcons again, their eyesight, how they're too far away to hear but still close enough to see us. They're the fastest birds in the world, I'm thinking, half-awake. *Zoom,* I'm thinking, *zoom.* The kid went somewhere. I wonder if I will see him again. Surely, the Californians will know I am here. If they didn't recognize me earlier, the hospital logs will alert them. A wounded person with the obvious marks of a grove worker—orange-stained hands, dark skin, and this denim shirt? They'll know. They have people. One of our groves must have slighted them somehow. With Californians, you can never tell; it could have been a murder, sure, or a rape or a kidnapping. One of us might have walked into the wrong grocery store. An apology wouldn't matter then. The Californians are more than terri-torial. In late-night meetings at the grove, some have asked aloud if the Californians are even human. My suspicions are confirmed when an old cleaning lady pushes her cart into my room and closes the door. Without speaking, she unhooks my leg from its pedestal and moves me into a wheelchair, raising the left footrest so that my leg lays horizontal to my lap. As she wheels me to the freight elevator, I hear familiar voices asking the nurse about any new patients with gunshot wounds. The elevator door closes, and I allow myself one long exhalation.

"Are you going to kill me?" I say, still doped into a stupor. When she doesn't respond, I try to say something about who I am and what I'll do to her and her family, and it comes out in a garble. I try again. I try to think of something to say. "Zoom," I say. "Zoom."

She nods. Maybe she doesn't speak English?

The door opens into a delivery bay, and the old woman steers me into the back of a tractor-trailer. Inside, a weak yellow light shines down on more than a dozen wounded men, all Floridian, some with as little as a bandaged arm and others who may already be dead. The old woman straps me against the wall. I'm staring at her as she closes the trailer door.

"Thank you," I say. The old lady just stands there. Her gaze stays with me after the door slams shut. It follows me as the truck begins to move, down the drive and out into the interstate. Part of me thinks she must still be staring, eyes on me from afar.

Shh. I can feel her now.

Inside the truck, rumors eat us alive. The other men may as well be retelling the same story. Only the details differ. Kidnapped. Identified. Escaping. Not all of them were picked up one by one like me; many were captured in groups while holding holiday parties. As far as these men know, they are the only survivors. Some say the war is over, that the Californians have won and our precious groves will burn and that we, marked by our orange-stained hands and denim shirts, will be hunted like animals. Others say it is mere retribution, that our side must have gained market share or the Californians lost production capacity, meaning they must restrict our own output to remain competitive. One man claims our masters in Florida and the masters of California are one and the same, that this state of war in which we have always existed is little more than a ruthless scheme to maximize the price an Average-Yet-Discriminating Grocery Shopper will tolerate in the local supermarket. We do not know for sure. We pass the time by asking for familiar faces, trading names, recalling tenuous connections, and searching for something that links us other than orange juice. Our conversations orbit these themes, and we cast our nets wider for some desperate connection. Two men believe they slept with the same woman in Austin, years apart. In the absence of anything else, this makes them almost brothers. I am jealous, but whether of their newfound fraternity or the touch of a woman, I cannot say for sure. The journey back to Florida takes a long time, and we must use back roads.

As we're driving through Georgia, something slams into the truck, and the trailer topples onto its left side, bouncing once, overturning those in wheelchairs and injuring those unlucky enough to duck and cover. One man wins the dark lottery of physics and circumstance—a heavy antique wheelchair breaks his skull. Dark blood seeps from the wound as he dies. I hear gunshots. I decide I will not die in this trailer and open the door, ignoring the pain in my foot, squirming from the rear of the truck and squinting in the dying afternoon light. I elbow through broken glass and cigarette butts, adjusting to the sunshine. When I look up, I see an Ingles.

Not just any Ingles. With a conviction I have never felt before or since, a faint voice whispers that this must be my Ingles, at 100 Fairview Road. I decide I will die crawling toward it, if die I must. Recalling the Bible passages my grandmother told me with the air of a campfire spook story, I feel I must by no means turn to look behind; whether the others make it from the truck or die, my task is not to save them. Whatever passes for my destiny must be in that store. Why else would I have been brought here, I who have killed eight human beings and more than a dozen Californians in our unending war to supply you with premium orange juice?

I have made the conclusion of all great men—that there is more to this world than accident.

As I drag myself toward the store, a red Toyota Tercel coasts past me, parking next to a row of shopping carts. A woman dressed for church emerges on her cell phone and gracefully steps over me, switching her purse from one hand to the other.

By the time I reach the automatic doors, three more people have walked around me, and the sound of gunshots dwindles. Whichever side won must be walking from corpse to corpse, dropping one last bullet into each man's head. Soon, they will see the missing wheelchair and note my absence. They will know where I am moving. They are not so stupid as to think an ordinary person would notice, much less help, someone who grows oranges for a living. We are as invisible as the rest of the poor. We have probably been in the same room together, you and I, and I looked enviously at your well-kept shoes from a corner. It must have been you. I'm crawling toward the entrance, dragging myself as you hurtle past and around and over. I swear I remember those shoes.

I gather my strength and lift myself into an electric shopping cart, the kind you can drive down the aisles. No one notices my erratic route, bumping over displays of cheese crackers and canned tomatoes, blinking back and forth into consciousness, cursing how orange juice is always kept on a far side of a grocery store. They're coming. I can hear them. They're fanning out in case the toppled crackers are a diversion. And you, Average-Yet-Discriminating Grocery Shopper, if you notice them at all, must assume that whomever they're pursuing deserves to be caught. I don't blame you. The Californians are tall and tan, and their sure gait matches their uniforms and posture. They exude authority, and I leave nothing but a lingering scent of citrus so faint it reminds you of a gas station bathroom. But the Californians have been taught to attack on sight and smell. I cannot fault them. If they do not catch me, they will surely die themselves. This has ever been an unforgiving business. They will kill me. I would do the same.

Do you occasionally feel a surge of goose bumps out of nowhere? They say it means someone has walked over your grave, but here's the truth: That someone is always someone like me, and we're not walking over the site of your future burial. We're careening into you and glancing off, often wounded and on the run. A woman shivers as I turn past her, falling out of the cart and skidding to a stop at aisle 15—dairy products, butter, orange juice, and eggs. Surely, all Ingles use the same layout, but again, somehow I know this is my Ingles. It reminds me of you, Average-Yet-Discriminating Grocery Shopper. I have imagined you here so many times, on the best and worst and most forgettable days of your life, pawing through one product or another but always drawn inevitably to me—to the bright orange promise this juice implies amid the pallid shelves of the dairy aisle.

I'm pulling myself up, my hands squishing into plastic-wrapped blocks of sharp cheddar, Monterey Jack, and mozzarella.

I'm pulling myself up to the second row of shelves, and I'm knocking away cartons of juice, their paper sides slippery from condensation. I hear the shuffle of footsteps and the shouts of the Californians and wonder if they will shoot me here, like this; and they're running toward me, and I'm reaching in, and my god, in this moment, I am you, Average-Yet-Discriminating Grocery Shopper; and you are me, and we are both this distance between us, and therefore, the hand reaching toward me—the unseen warmth against my bloodied fingertips—must be my own, by which I mean yours, by which I mean we can never fear death in a moment like this, orbiting, turning in widening gyres, moving in circles around a world that never ends.

Contributors

Camille Alexa was born in California, raised in Texas, schooled in Toronto, and currently lives in the Pacific Northwest, down the street from a volcano. Her stories have appeared in Alfred Hitchcock's and Ellery Queen's mystery magazines, *Fantasy, Machine of Death,* and *Imaginarium 2012: The Best Canadian Speculative Writing.* Her short fiction collection, *Push of the Sky,* was an Endeavour Award finalist and a Powell's Books Science Fiction Book Club reading selection. More about her work and about her superexciting supercoedited superanthology, *Masked Mosaic: Canadian Super Stories,* at www.camillealexa.com or on Twitter @camillealexa.

David Boop is a Denver-based single dad, returning college student, temp worker, and author. He's had one novel, the sci-fi/noir *She Murdered Me with Science,* and over thirty short stories published. The latest, an urban sci-fi, appears in *Aliens among Us.* He tours the country attending conventions and speaking on his specialty genre, weird Westerns. His hobbies include film noir, anime, the blues, and Mayan history. You can find out more at DavidBoop.com or Facebook.com/dboop.updates.

Ben Bowlin was born in Nashville; his family hails from the Melungeon haunts and hollers of Eastern Tennessee. He's lived in Atlanta and Quetzaltenango, where he investigated the worship of a local deity named Maximón (or Hermano San Simón to his friends). Swing by @BenBowlin or BenBowlin.org if you feel like saying hello, and as always, thank you for reading.

Meriah Crawford is a writer, an assistant professor at Virginia Commonwealth University, and a private investigator. After the Louisa quake, Meriah spent hours helping her mother clean up the tremendous mess at her home in Mineral. Though the USGS and others provided an enormous amount of really valuable information during the aftermath, Meriah felt it was important to write this story to set the record straight at last. Meriah's published writing includes short stories, a variety of nonfiction work, and a poem about semicolons. For more information, visit www.mlcrawford.com. Or if you buy her a glass of port, she'll tell you some of the stories she can't put into writing.

Janice Croom has been writing for fifteen years. In 2013, she will release the *Kadence MacBride* mystery series online. African American couple Kadence and Terrence, best friends since college, have supported each other through twenty years of failed marriages and dead-end relationships. Despite their strong mutual attraction, they've been unwilling to risk their friendship for a chance at love—until now. They find that friends really do make the best lovers and would be well on their way to "happily ever after" if they could just stop stumbling over dead bodies. To learn more about Janice's writing, visit http://janicecroom.wordpress.com.

Chris Dezarn is a writer from the American South. Dezarn writes in a variety of genres, but his is a new voice making noise in the world of horror. Dezarn's twisted tales are usually dark, often shocking, sometimes humorous, but always entertaining and demanding attention. Dezarn is just getting started and hopes you'll join him for more trips to the dark side. Dezarn currently dwells in East Tennessee, where he spends his time thinking up ways to induce nightmares.

Lara Ek is an English teacher living in Harbin, China, who graduated from George Mason University with degrees in creative writing and

Chinese and has previously been published in *Crossed Genres, Nanoism,* and *Volition.*

Megan Engelhardt is a lapsed librarian who knows better than to make crossroad deals. She has previously been published in *Daily Science Fiction, The Drabblecast,* and *Crossed Genres,* among others. She can be found online at www.megengelhardt.com and on Twitter @MadMerryMeg.

Sherry Fasano lives in Rembert, South Carolina, with her husband and dog named Daisy. She has been writing family stories and fiction for several years. Daisy is her #1 critic.

Laura Haddock lives in Memphis, Tennessee, with her husband, two technically grown-up daughters, and an assortment of odd animals. She grew up in a family full of old folks, and their stories and experiences inspire much of her work. Laura's stories can be found online on Postcard Shorts and SQ Mag. When she's not writing about ghosts and aliens and such, she volunteers as a moderator on My Writers Circle and works a desk job to keep the lights on. Laura often has a faraway blank look on her face because she's busy thinking up new stories.

Michael Hodges lives in Chicagoland but often dreams of the Northern Rockies. Camping and animal nut. Represented by Laura Wood at FinePrint Literary. His two most recent short stories are "Grangy" at *AE: The Canadian Science Fiction Review* and "Seven Fish for Sarah" at *Penumbra Magazine.* You can always read more at MichaelHodgesFiction.com. His Twitter handle is @MichaelBHodges.

Wenonah Lyon is a retired anthropologist, born in Atlanta and currently living in the UK. She has published short prose and poetry in *In Posse Review, Quantum Muse, Flashquake, Gator Springs Gazette, The Dead Mule School of Southern Literature, New Maps, Ajax,* and other online and print publications. Some of this fiction has been reprinted (*City-Lit* series, Berlin) and sold for audio downloading (Escape Pod). Links to some of her published fiction and nonfiction can be found on her website, www.wenonahlyon.com.

Peter Mehren, a Californian living in Toronto, could have been a son of the Confederacy had an ancestor not taken some relatives and some slaves and moved from Alabama to California. Peter's beautiful and brilliant wife, Kay, has enabled him to be happy while indulging hobbies which some might have considered jobs: teaching, editing, acting, writing, managing farms while in the Peace Corps, managing offices, and so on. Neither Peter nor Kay has, to our knowledge, seen a ghost; but we did have an article in *Fate Magazine* about a definitely haunted house where Kay worked, and we've heard a few ghosts, and Peter had his head flicked by something where nothing could have been—probably his late mother wanting him to get a haircut. He acted in a docudrama, a film called *The Wicca Tapes: Ghosts*, and in a ghost-plagued and commercially unsuccessful pilot for a series about haunted places. He has sold non-fiction, fiction, and semifiction to several publications, an activity he continues to pursue.

Kristina R. Mosley lives in Kensett, Arkansas, a small town that provides a great deal of writing inspiration. Her work has been featured in numerous publications, including *Scifaikuest, Tales from the Grave, Eschatology,* and *MicroHorror.* She blogs from time to time at kristinarmosley.blogspot.com, and she tweets too often at twitter.com/elstupacabra.

Erin Mundy is a student at University of North Georgia (formerly North Georgia College and State University) majoring in English. Her previous works include papers for her classes, but this is her first published story. When not studying in the hopes that she will graduate soon, she enjoys being a leader at North Georgia's BCM. Having grown up with Lake Lanier in her backyard, she cares about the lake and the people who love it.

Steve Newton is an associate professor of English at William Paterson University in Wayne, New Jersey. He was a Fulbright Scholar in 2005–2006 at the Institute for American Studies at the University of Graz in Austria. As a younger man, he pumped gas in Alamosa, Colorado, drove a forklift in a cement factory in Cleveland, was a night shift janitor at the Grand Ole Opry, and one memorable Christmas was Santa Claus in a shopping mall outside Nashville.

Daniel Powell teaches a variety of writing courses at a small college in Northeast Florida. His work has appeared in *Redstone Science Fiction, Well Told Tales, Brain Harvest, Leading Edge magazine, Everyday Weirdness, Something Wicked, Dead but Dreaming 2,* and *Weber: The Contemporary West.* Visit him at www.danielwpowell.blogspot.com.

Lewis Powell IV is the creator and writer of the *Southern Spirit Guide* blog (http://southernspiritguide.blogspot.com), a blog covering the ghosts and hauntings of the American South. A native Georgian, Lewis is an actor, writer, and researcher with a BFA in theater from Columbus State University, Columbus, Georgia. He was also the contributing editor of *In Order of Appearance*, a history of the famous performers who have graced the stage of Columbus' legendary and haunted Springer Opera House.

Jay Rogers was born in the Tri-State area of the Southwest Ozarks in 1935. His first decade, he was told, "Hush up 'n' listen" to the family's storytellers. He was in awe of those folks but never imagined "oral recitin'" in his destiny. He told his kids those tales as they were growing up, and they "begat" more kids who heard the tales. The storytelling and the "begattin'" continued until the supper table couldn't seat all the generations if they showed up at the same time, so Jay began writing the stories for all. Someone dared him to submit a written story to a publisher who might accept it, which would mark Jay as a professional writer. He commenced "rootin' around the trough" and chose one called "The Spook Light." Long story short: He did. They did. Now he are one.

Herb Shallcross graduated from Drexel in 2007 with a BS in psychology and a certificate in writing and publishing. His poems and stories have appeared online at *Apiary Magazine* and *Eclectic Flash* and in anthologies from Elektrik Milk Bath Press and the Bards Initiative. Herb lives in Queens with his wonderful wife.

Josh Strnad is a small-town guy from North Carolina, a lawn-equipment wrangler, an audiobook addict, and a sand sculpture master craftsman. When not guzzling hot tea and typing stories on his battered desktop computer, he dabbles in filmmaking, writing music, and drawing cartoons. He's currently working his way through graduate studies to become a high school English teacher, writing his second novel, and illustrating his children's book in his copious spare time. Check him out on Facebook or at www.joshstrnad.com.

Sean Taylor is an award-winning writer of stories. He grew up telling lies, and he got pretty good at it, so now he writes them into full-blown adventures for comic books, graphic novels, magazines, book anthologies, and novels. He makes stuff up for money, and he writes it down for fun. He's a lucky fellow that way. He's best known for his work on the best-selling *Gene Simmons Dominatrix* comic book series from IDW Publishing and Simmons Comics Group. He has also written comics for TV properties such as the top-rated Oxygen Network series *Bad Girls Club*. His other forays into fiction include such realms as steampunk, pulp, young adult, fantasy, superheroes, sci-fi, and even samurai frogs on horseback (seriously, don't laugh), and he has appeared in short story collections alongside such writing heroes as Joe Lansdale and Nancy Collins. However, his favorite contribution to the world will be as the writer/editor who invented the genre and coined the term "hookerpunk." For more information (and mug shots), visit www.taylorverse.com.

Ken Teutsch is a writer, performer, and videographer, born and raised in southern Arkansas.

DL Thurston lives in Annandale, Virginia, with his wife, daughter, and cats. His stories can also be found in the *Steam Works* and *Memory Eater* anthologies. He is a proud member of the Cat Vacuuming Society of Northern Virginia and can be found through his blog, DLThurston.com.

Tim Westover lives in suburban Atlanta. Born in the north, educated in England, and a frequent visitor to Russia, he found his home in the North Georgia mountains, where his first novel, *Auraria* (QW Publishers, 2012), is set. In addition to writing, Westover busies himself with programming, playing the clawhammer banjo, and raising his one-year-old daughter to be a modern American eccentric. He is also an established writer in the International Language Esperanto; his short story collection *Marvirinistrato* (Mermaid Street) was published in 2009, and his stories appear in translation in the anthology *Star in a Night Sky* (Francis Boutle Publishers, 2012). Visit his blog at www.timwestover.com.

52374086R00120

Made in the USA
Lexington, KY
12 September 2019